SF IO
us

✔ **KT-598-901**

Tears tracked down her face. "Look, Jason. Our baby is so…"

He didn't have the words either. Instead he wiped away her tears with his thumb, then on instinct followed with his lips.

A lump of tenderness rose in his throat, followed by a huge mass of protectiveness in his heart.

It was this kind of emotion that made a doctor miss important signs and symptoms. He worked hard to get himself under control, even though the warmth of Stephanie's hand distracted him.

Their child. One father. One mother. One child.

And together the three of them made up a family. The concept sent a shiver down his spine and raised the hairs on his arms.

Dear Reader

When I sat down to write this story it was as if I'd just stepped off the elevator at the Sheffield Memorial Paediatric Diagnostics Floor to see Dr Jason Drake, with all his intensity, in a locked stare with Dr Stephanie Montclair—his equal in every way.

Frankly, I just held on for the ride as they battled illness along with their attraction to each other.

A calling to the medical profession is an emotional pull born of sympathy and nurturing. Yet doctors, particularly those who work with children, must not become overwhelmed with emotion to the point where they cannot apply medical science and logic. It's a struggle to find that balance, and it can take a great toll on the spirit. But not bearing that load alone is what this story is all about.

Dr Jason Drake and Dr Stephanie Montclair find respite in each other's arms, but they need more. Will proud, strong heiress Stephanie risk heartache when Jason proposes to share responsibility for her professional burdens as well as for her unborn baby? Can the stoic and brilliant Jason accept the emotional healing Stephanie offers to sustain him through the trials of his profession as well as the tragedy of his past? And, when these decisions take a life-or-death turn, will love conquer all?

These two dynamic doctors kept me on the edge of my seat from beginning to end. I hope you enjoy reading their story as much as I enjoyed sharing it with you. Let me know!

Connie

www.ConnieCox.com

THE BABY
WHO SAVED
DR CYNICAL

BY
CONNIE COX

First published in Great Britain 2012
by Mills & Boon, an imprint of Harlequin (UK) Limited.
Large Print edition 2012
Harlequin (UK) Limited, Eton House,
18-24 Paradise Road, Richmond, Surrey TW9 1SR

© Connie Cox 2012

ISBN: 978 0 263 22469 6

LP

Harlequin (UK) policy is to use papers that aɪ
natural, renewable and recyclable products aɪ
from wood grown in sustainable forests. The logging
and manufacturing process conform to the legal
environmental regulations of the country of origin.

Printed and bound in Great Britain
by CPI Antony Rowe, Chippenham, Wiltshire

Connie Cox has loved Harlequin Mills and Boon® romances since she was a young teen. Now to be a Mills and Boon® author is a fantasy come to life. By training, Connie is an electrical engineer. Through her first job, working on nuclear scanners and other medical equipment, she gained a unique perspective into the medical world. She is fascinated by the inner strength of medical professionals, who must balance emotional compassion with stoic logic, and is honoured to showcase the passion of these dedicated professionals through her own passion of writing. Married to the boy-next-door, Connie is the proud mother of one terrific daughter and son-in-law, and one precocious dachshund.

Connie would love to hear from you. Visit her website at www.ConnieCox.com

This is Connie's first book
for M&B Medical™ Romance.
Look out for more from her coming soon!

This book is dedicated to Sonia, sister of my heart, who always believes in me, and to Amy and Winnie, who follow their bliss and inspire me to do the same.

CHAPTER ONE

SHE'D done it. She'd sold Dr. Jason Drake's reputation for three million dollars and a closed case.

As Director of Diagnostics, Dr. Stephanie Montclair had agreed to pay off the family's wrongful death claim, with Dr. Jason Drake's name on the line as the attending physician and no fault levied against Sheffield Memorial Hospital.

"We all tried our best to keep that precious little boy alive. Dr. Drake stayed up here three days straight trying to save little Isaac," Stephanie offered in token protest to the ring of lawyers that surrounded her desk.

"You're doing the right thing," the chief legal counselor reassured her. "A good prosecuting attorney would have a judge and jury in tears inside three minutes flat. Even if we were to win the suit in the end, Sheffield Memorial can't risk the prolonged negative publicity. And if Dr. Drake is called to the stand, with his brash manner, we can't predict how he'll come across."

Reluctantly, Stephanie agreed. Jason was a great doctor—one of the best—but he'd never seen the need to sugarcoat his words.

"There has to be a better way. Sanction me instead."

"Not an option, Dr. Montclair. The board would never approve it, and rightly so," one of the lawyers said. "That move could put the whole department in jeopardy."

The case had been heartbreaking. In conjunction with Diagnostics, Sheffield's Neonatal Unit had tried scores of unorthodox methods to keep the premature infant alive, many of them beyond the edge of convention, only to have the grieving parents lash out at the hospital to try to ease their pain.

That little Isaac's parents were high-profile celebrities hadn't helped. The grief-stricken couple had threatened to call in every publicity connection they had if Sheffield Memorial didn't take action against the culprit who'd killed their baby.

Stephanie could understand the parents' anguish. Although she'd only known about her own baby a few short weeks, the thought of losing that tiny life inside her sent heavy waves of dread through her heart.

Still, she and the lawyers couldn't make them

understand there was nothing Jason or anyone else could have done better.

And now the hospital's reputation was in danger. As a small, private research and teaching hospital, Sheffield Memorial kept its doors open only through grants and goodwill.

Dr. Wilkins chimed in. "Stephanie, the board recommendation to name Dr. Drake in the lawsuit is the least harmful action we can take for the greater good. Dr. Drake might have his shortcomings, but he's one of the top diagnostic physicians in the world. His stellar professional standing can take the hit with no lasting, detrimental effect. That's why we shell out the big bucks for his malpractice insurance."

Not only was Wilkins the board's treasurer, he was a family friend who had attended her christening. He knew her Achilles' heel.

"We've already seen a drop in patient referrals. A messy court case along with a star-studded media circus would call our accreditations into question and jeopardize critical funding. We would have to turn away sick children who need us."

Before she could waver, she signed on the dotted line. Each of the hospital's team of lawyers stood and shook her hand, sealing the deal. She would be washing that hand as soon as possible.

As they left her office, Dr. Wilkins hung back from the others. "The board and I were worried you'd let your personal relationship with Dr. Drake influence your decision. They will be pleased to learn you had no qualms about putting Sheffield Memorial first."

Stephanie clearly heard the unspoken threat behind his words, despite the fact the hospital was named after her maternal great-grandfather.

Doctors ran on both sides of the family. Her mother was a cardiologist. Her father an endocrinologist. Both sat on the hospital board. Although if a newcomer had suggested Stephanie had been appointed to her current position of Director of Pediatric Diagnostics because of who she was, instead of what she did, she hoped any of the hospital personnel would be quick to disabuse them. Stephanie worked day and night to be twice as competent as any other department head and prove she'd earned her position.

Then again, those who knew her staff didn't envy her. She was the only department head who could handle Jason Drake.

"Tell them not to worry. I would never put the hospital at risk for personal reasons." She hesitated to add more, but everyone on the Diagnostics floor already knew anyway. "Dr. Drake and I aren't together anymore."

"The board will be glad to hear it." Whether that was a comment on her loyalty to the hospital or her relationship with Dr. Drake or both, Stephanie didn't know. She only knew that, even though she'd effectively besmirched and betrayed Jason, she had made the right decision. So why did it feel so wrong?

Her stomach lurched, as if her baby were protesting Mommy's ill treatment of Daddy. Yes, the deal she'd finagled left a very sour taste in her mouth.

Outside the patient's open door, Stephanie stopped to gather her thoughts. She could see that Jason was already inside the room.

In accordance with the terms of the settlement, Stephanie would sit in on this case and every other case Jason picked up for the next six months. It was a mixed blessing that the bad publicity they'd already received had resulted in fewer patients checking into Sheffield Memorial. She wasn't sure how she would have handled the extra duties along with her normal responsibilities. But at least the morning sickness was letting up now.

Her involvement in his cases hadn't been an issue in the past. In fact, even though her administrative duties had limited her patient load, Jason had always invited her in on cases he'd thought would interest her. Hopefully he would continue to welcome her after he learned of the lawsuit.

As he paid little attention to any hospital business outside of medicine, she was counting on him shrugging off the deal as a necessary evil and continuing on as normal.

Only with the compromises she'd had to make it wouldn't be quite as normal as she would have liked, though she would try to make it as painless as possible for both of them.

As usual, Jason wore scrubs, although the other diagnosticians wore business attire and lab coats. On his six-feet-four frame the drawstring pants and boxy shirt took nothing away from his lean build, kept hard with hiking and white-water rafting.

He needed a haircut. His spiky dark blond hair went out of control almost as fast as his mouth did. How many times had she finger-combed those strands into place after making love?

One too many, apparently.

Originally they had agreed to keep it casual. She had avoided relationships in the past, not wanting to take her focus off her climb up the medical ladder, but Jason Drake had seemed perfect. Remote.

Stoic. Yet highly sensual and with no strings attached. Perfect for her first intentionally cavalier relationship.

When Jason had seemed reluctant to talk about himself, his roots, his past, his reticence had only helped her stay detached—at least that was what she'd told herself. She had gotten exactly what she'd thought she wanted. But now she couldn't stop herself from wanting more.

She'd thought something special was developing between them, but now she understood she'd mistaken sexual attraction for an emotional connection.

No, she'd never meant to fall for him. He certainly hadn't made the same mistake with her. Jason didn't do emotions.

Now she was certain they had no future together. Not even for the sake of the baby. They might have if he'd bothered to show up for dinner that night, but she'd not been important enough to derail his plans—again.

At three and a half months, she would be showing soon. She should try again to tell Jason about the baby. He had a right to know, even if she didn't expect anything from him.

If only he were daddy material.

* * *

Damn. He hated these cases.

The little dark-haired girl wasn't quite four yet. She had big brown eyes that looked up to him to make her feel better.

He flipped through her chart, noting all the tests she'd gone through. The kid had been poked by more needles than a porcupine had. She couldn't understand.

Stay objective. Sympathy doesn't fix anyone.

First the baby boy, Isaac, and now this little girl was really getting to him. He was going soft. It didn't help that this was the anniversary of his brother's death—which should be the perfect reminder to keep his emotions out of the equation.

He needed a stress-reliever.

One good night in Stephanie's bed would fix him right up. Her, too.

Medicine wasn't the only thing he took pride in.

He still didn't understand what had happened. It was only a missed dinner date, and they'd both agreed at the beginning to keep things casual. Their careers were too important for anything more serious, which suited Jason perfectly. He had vowed on his brother's grave that he would never, ever lose himself in a relationship again.

Even if Stephanie didn't want to be intimate they could share a meal, talk, enjoy each other's company. Although he'd never been lonely before, since their breakup his evenings stretched into long, empty, sleepless hours to be endured before morning, when he could get back to his work.

He gave a tight nod to the girl's mother. "The test results are in. It's not multiple sclerosis."

Her mother gave him a protective version of her daughter's smile. "That's good. What's next?"

Automatically he compared the mother's features to her daughter's, looking for clues to an inheritable condition.

The father wasn't in the picture. How could any man look at himself in the mirror after deserting his own child? And a developmentally disabled child at that?

"We're still ruling out various forms of muscular dystrophy. We're testing muscular DNA samples, which may tell us something and may not. I'm not going to do a nerve conduction velocity test until I have to. It's rather uncomfortable and I don't think Maggie will understand." He should really run the test and get it over with, but Maggie had been through a lot lately and he might get his answer in a less invasive way.

Yes, he was definitely getting soft, and it was affecting his logic. Not good. For him or his patients.

His attention was diverted by Stephanie coming up behind them.

Jason would recognize that walk anywhere. Steady, confident and competent. In her customary high heels, she reached his chin. He only had to dip his head to meet her, mouth-to-mouth.

She walked with purpose. She did everything with purpose.

Directness was one of the qualities he admired about her—along with her body, her hair, her smell. He admired everything about her except her decision to break it off with him.

Her long, straight mink-brown hair was gathered into a low ponytail today.

It had been four weeks and two days since he'd freed it from its bindings and wrapped it around him like a waterfall in the privacy of her bedroom.

"I'll be joining you on this case, Dr. Drake."

"You're the boss." Not that he answered to any man—or woman. He knew his purpose in life. Grabbing people back from the abyss of death had nothing to do with administrative rules or regulations.

Still, she was good at what she did: juggling patient care, internal politics and financial budgets. He had to admit his life ran much more smoothly with her in charge.

What was different about her lately?

Did her eyes look deeper? Her face rounder? Was she glowing? She might have put on a few pounds. He couldn't be certain with her open lab coat covering her button-down shirt and straight fitted skirt. If so, they looked good on her.

"I'm Dr. Montclair." Stephanie introduced herself, giving equal attention to daughter and mother.

"Please call me Anne, and this is Maggie." Maggie's mom stood and shook hands.

Stephanie crouched down to Maggie's eye level as the child sat in her bed. "How are you today, Maggie?"

Maggie looked past Stephanie and stuffed her doll's hand into her mouth.

"I'm going to listen to your heart, okay?" She unwrapped her stethoscope from her lab coat pocket and hung it around her neck.

At Sheffield Memorial it was policy that each doctor on a case would check vitals and make independent assessments. Attention to such details was one of the key factors that made Sheffield Memorial such a renowned teaching and research hospital, even if it was much smaller than most public institutions.

Despite Stephanie's cheerful tone and slow movements, Maggie whimpered and drew back.

Anne spoke up. "She only lets Dr. Drake do that."

Jason frowned. He hadn't realized. Maggie had no reason to like him or trust him. He hadn't asked for that. He only wanted to assess her symptoms, identify the problem and fix it.

Stephanie stepped back. "What if I listen to Mom's heart first?"

Maggie shook her head. An emphatic no.

Anne stroked her daughter's hair to calm her. "Could Dr. Montclair listen to Dr. Drake's heart, then?"

The child grinned around the doll in her mouth.

He and Stephanie hadn't touched, even to brush hands, since their break-up. The anticipation of her hands on him made his skin quiver.

He took a step back. "If we need to forgo this I can debrief you with all Maggie's vitals as well as her current condition before the diagnostics meeting, Dr. Montclair."

"I appreciate that. Now, let's set a good example for Maggie and try the stethoscope." Stephanie fitted the earpieces and waggled her finger at Jason to come closer. "Stand still and take a deep breath, Dr. Drake."

When she placed her hand on his chest, the single layer of material between them did nothing to stop a spark arcing between her hand and his heart.

He concentrated on keeping his heart-rate steady but failed miserably. He could feel the pounding in his ears. What kind of example would he set for Maggie if he grabbed Stephanie and bolted from the room with her at her very proper touch?

Stephanie was having no problem being steady, cool and in control.

Using great discipline, he controlled his breathing, steadily in and out. His professional reputation was at stake.

Stephanie gave him a worried look but said nothing.

Finally, she dropped her hands and turned to Maggie. "Your turn?"

Aside from a grimace, the girl didn't protest this time.

"Now let me take your pulse, Dr. Drake." She held out her hand for his wrist.

No sense in fighting the inevitable. When she asked, he could deny her nothing.

Her warm, open palm held him as captive as a set of handcuffs. The pad of her fingers rocked back and forth until she found the throbbing in his wrist.

Would she notice if his heart skipped a beat or two?

"Thank you, Dr. Drake." She turned back to

Maggie, who appeared to be avidly looking to the left of their little charade. "Your turn, Maggie. May I hold your arm?"

To Jason's amazement, Maggie held out her wrist. This was the first response she'd made to anyone's request since she'd been hospitalized. From the sudden alertness in her mother's eyes, this was unexpected for Anne, too.

Stephanie found the girl's pulse and counted.

"Thank you, Maggie." The moment Stephanie released her arm Maggie put it under the covers.

"Perfect," she told the girl. "Now, let's check ears and eyes. Dr. Drake, if you'll sit, please?" She pointed to the visitor's chair beside the bed.

Maggie scrambled to turn herself onto her side and peer through the railings to watch. Observing and analyzing Maggie's movements helped distract Jason from the intimacy of his own examination. If Maggie could so easily pull her legs under her and twist sideways, why couldn't she walk? She had once been able to run around the house without hesitation. How did her late ambulatory development factor in?

"Ears first." Stephanie leaned over him, her breasts inches from his mouth. He swallowed hard to keep from drooling.

Her featherlight touch tickled the rim of his ear.

As Stephanie leaned close to look, her sweet breath warmed his neck.

Every primal cell in his body screamed for him to pick her up, throw her over his shoulder and take her back to his lair. For Maggie's sake he kept himself still and unresponsive, although his clenched palms had begun to sweat.

"That didn't bother you a bit, did it, Dr. Drake?"

"No, not at all." He forced the lie past his gritted teeth.

"Now, let's take a look at your eyes."

There was no way Jason could hide the dilation of his pupils—a physiological reaction to his desire. To distract himself, he silently listed the noble gasses from the periodic table while congratulating himself on his own noble restraint.

Stephanie's intense scrutiny made him want to wince away, but her hand on his shoulder held him still. Once she was satisfied with what she saw she released him. He sank back into the chair, so tense every nerve-ending twanged like over-tightened guitar strings.

Stephanie showed no signs of being affected at all. As if they were nothing but colleagues and had never been lovers. As if he'd never made her scream his name into the night, or washed breakfast dishes beside her in the morning.

What had he done besides miss a dinner date or two? Duty had called. She'd grown up in a doctors' household. Surely she understood? It had to be something more.

"Your turn, Maggie." Stephanie moved from chair to bedside.

Maggie began to protest by grunting, and waving the hand that didn't hold her doll, but when Jason enfolded her fluttering hand in his he settled down and let Stephanie shine a light into her eyes as she stared at the wall past her mother.

"All done." Stephanie stuck the small light into her lab coat pocket. "You're a very brave girl, Maggie."

At her name, Maggie slid her glance past Stephanie to rest slightly to the right. She held out her doll in an obvious invitation to be friends.

Careful to avoid the doll's wet chewed hand, Stephanie took the ratty-haired toy and cradled it in her arms, giving the honor proper tribute. She gave the doll a pat and reverently tucked it into bed beside Maggie. "Thank you, Maggie. I'll come back and visit soon."

Stephanie would be a good mother. Jason's thoughts startled him so much he stood abruptly. He'd never thought of motherhood and Stephanie Montclair in the same breath before.

She had a demanding job and a busy social schedule. How could she add motherhood to the mix, even if she wanted to? And then there was the little issue of who would father her child.

He had the strangest urge to volunteer.

First his disturbing emotional reaction to his patients and now this? No, he was not cut out to be a family man, much as he might daydream about it. He had enough past history to prove he did more harm than good in that role. He really needed to make arrangements for a few days off soon…

"Diagnostics meeting starts in five minutes." He walked to the door to get Stephanie moving in that direction.

"If there's anything I or my staff can do to make your stay more comfortable, let me know," Stephanie said to Maggie's mother, sounding like the concierge of an expensive hotel. Was she really that worried about the fall-off of patients?

She probably was. Sheffield Memorial was her family's legacy—something she took very seriously. There was nothing she wouldn't do to make it thrive. Next thing he knew she would be sending in staff to put mints on the patients' pillows.

Drake couldn't fault her. If he'd had a legacy of any sort he might feel the same. But mongrels like him had no birthright to speak of. And the heritage he *did* have was better off left unspoken.

As soon as the door latched behind him, she stopped him with a hand to his arm, sending tingles to the soles of his feet. "Before we talk about the girl, I want you to get a physical. Your heart rate is too fast and your blood pressure is elevated."

"I'm fine."

"That's a direct order. Got it?"

Protesting wouldn't get him back on her good side. "Fine. I'll get it checked out. I didn't know you cared."

"Of course I care. This hospital is in enough trouble with the media without one of our physicians dropping dead in the hallway because he neglected his own health."

"Your concern is touching." He put distance between them, but his arm still tingled where her hand had been.

Stephanie used all her will-power to keep from reaching out and pulling him back to her.

She craved the vibrations he sent through her when he touched her, the deep-seated sense of wellbeing and protection he gave her whenever he was near. But he had proved to her too many times that it was a false sense of security.

She couldn't count on him to keep a dinner date, much less a vow of happily-ever-after.

Stephanie picked up her pace, putting even more distance between them. She didn't need him, and neither did her baby.

A wave of exhaustion tinged with queasiness hit her, pressing on her shoulders and dragging at her heels. Normal, her obstetrician had promised her. It should pass soon.

Like a good Montclair, Stephanie soldiered on.

She would need to tell her parents soon.

They were so conservative. Telling them about her unplanned baby would disappoint them at first. Not only was she unwed, she was a *doctor*, for heaven's sake. She should know how to prevent pregnancy.

Where once she would have whole-heartedly agreed with them, she now had a more sympathetic view. Accidents happened—even to medical professionals.

And this was a happy accident. She already loved her unborn child beyond measure.

Her parents and grandparents would support her in the end, even if they weren't totally happy to do so.

The Montclairs and the Sheffields stuck together, putting on a united front. They always had. In fact,

Stephanie felt confident that once they were over the shock of their dateless daughter being pregnant they would be thrilled at having a successor to carry on the family name—something her father perpetually worried about.

Her child would grow up knowing only respect and her unconditional love, no matter what anyone thought about his or her parentage. She would make sure of it.

Her child would be the center of her universe.

Yes, Stephanie was positive her child would lack for nothing except a father.

"Stephanie, are you all right?" Jason asked.

They had paused outside the conference room. When had they stopped walking? Preoccupation and distraction seemed to be another symptom of her pregnancy lately.

"I'm fine. Just fine," she snapped at him.

"You're pale." He ran a finger down her cheek—way too intimate for their present circumstances. "And clammy. And you have a faraway look in your eyes."

"I've got a lot on my mind."

"The lawsuit?"

"That's an issue I can't discuss with you right now." Not until the board signed off on her decision. That would probably happen sometime this evening, during the Montclair-Sheffield fundraiser, with board members discreetly disappearing into a private alcove to affix their signatures to the document that would blemish Jason's reputation.

But it was too late for second thoughts.

Soldier on, Stephanie.

Through the partially open blinds of the conference room she could see her diagnostic staff assembled. "They're waiting on us."

"Stephanie, if there's anything I can do to help—"

His offer surprised her.

Too soon she would have the unfortunate duty of telling him how the hospital he had devoted his whole life to was selling him out.

Yes, he would be well compensated for his involuntary sacrifice, but the board didn't understand. Jason didn't do what he did for money. He did it out of passion.

Stephanie knew she was the only one who understood the passion Jason hid beneath his cynically stoic exterior.

All he had to do was brush against her to remind her.

"After you." He held the door open for her, briefly trailing his fingertips on the small of her back to guide her through.

His gray eyes smoldered before he banked the fire, but she'd seen the desire that flickered there. And had felt a responding spark in herself—a spark that could all too easily be fanned into a full-blown inferno.

All vestiges of nausea and lethargy fled at his touch.

They were so good together. Maybe if...

No, it was too late for second thoughts.

CHAPTER TWO

JASON saw that Dr. Riser and Dr. Phillips had already seated themselves at the table with a cup of coffee each.

He turned to the kitchenette that housed a small microwave and refrigerator along with a pair of electric burners. One burner held a pot of brewed coffee, but Stephanie preferred tea.

Filling the extra pot with water, he put it on the burner to boil.

"It's rather warm in here, isn't it?" Stephanie began to peel off her lab coat.

Her skin was now flushed with healthy color instead of holding that pallor her worry had caused her. She really needed to get away—with him. A little time in his mountain cabin on his faux fur rug would fix her right up.

"Let me help you." Jason stepped toward her to help—out of politeness, but mostly out of the desire to touch her again. He yearned for that zing they created between them whenever they made contact, and couldn't keep himself from trying to recreate it whenever he had the chance.

But she shrugged away his outstretched hand as she hung the lab coat on the rack near the door.

Yes, her curves were definitely curvier.

As she slid into her office chair she picked up her glasses, anchored them low on the bridge of her nose and looked over the top at him. Did she know how that prim and proper look set him on fire? Was she teasing him on purpose?

He hoped so, but doubted it.

Since that fateful night two weeks ago, when he'd got caught up in his work and had to cancel their dinner date, she had rebuffed every move he'd made. He set the steeping cup of tea in front of her.

"No, thank you. I'm cutting down on caffeine." She shoved it back to him. "Now, tell me what's going on with little Maggie."

Jason took a sip of the tea himself, although it was too sweet for his taste. Then he stood and pointed to the whiteboard that listed symptoms and possible diagnoses and drew a line through multiple sclerosis. "The child is average in both weight and height. Reduced muscle tone, delayed development, lack of speech, yet good appetite and no fever. These symptoms aren't new. But after walking for a year and a half she now seems to have forgotten how. Dr. Montclair, what are your observations?"

Stephanie traced an invisible circle on the table. Her hands always moved as she processed. "Her vitals are good, all within the normal range. Her palm is warm. Not clammy or cold. Her grip is weak. Her fingernails are thin and flaky. And she has the longest eyelashes for a child of her age I've ever seen."

Fingernails and eyelashes. Only Stephanie had noticed the obvious. Added to the clues he'd already put together, a suspicion began to form in his mind.

Damn it, she looked different. Was she dating someone else?

Focus, Drake, he told himself. Mentally, he considered and discarded possible diagnoses.

"Anyone else have something to add?" he challenged his diagnostics team.

"She's obsessed with that doll," Dr. Phillips said. Dr. Phillips was the youngest and the chattiest, but her expertise in toxicology made her invaluable.

Like a parrot on her shoulder, Dr. Riser nodded in concurrence.

Dr. Riser had been doing a lot of that lately, instead of presenting his own ideas. Jason's team had been picked with great care, but even the best partnerships became stale after a while. And Jason hadn't picked Riser. The board had.

Dr. Riser was a neurosurgeon the hospital had brought in for an undisclosed salary. He regularly moonlighted for the neurology department.

The respiratory/pulmonary member of the group was missing today. Personal business, he'd said. Job interview, the rumor mill said. He was looking for a position with a higher success rate than their department.

Diagnostics was a last-ditch effort after all the other medical personnel had given up. Often the diagnosis came too late, or the patient couldn't be treated. Pediatric diagnostics was hard on the ego as well as the soul if a doctor valued his success rate over saving individual lives.

Stephanie answered Dr. Phillips. "Wouldn't you be fixated on your favorite toy, too? Surrounded by strangers, you'd be clinging to the few constants in your life."

He could always count on her to bring in the human aspect of a case. His team was becoming too narrowly focused, echoing his weaknesses as well as his strengths. Stephanie was exactly who he needed on this case. *And in his bed.*

No. He did *not* need Stephanie Montclair in his

bed. He *wanted* her in his bed, but he didn't *need* her there.

What he needed was focus. Stephanie made that damned hard. He was fascinated by this strong, sexy, intelligent woman.

He looked around at the assembled doctors, his gaze deliberately sliding past Stephanie.

Turning Dr. Phillips' observation on its side, he challenged, "Did anyone notice Maggie also chewed the sleeve of her nightgown and the edge of her blanket? Is it that she wants the doll, or does she just want to put something in her mouth?"

Drs Phillips and Riser easily nodded their agreement. Jason scowled, exasperated. He didn't need any yes-men. Or yes-women. He needed independent thinkers. Loyal accord didn't diagnose patients.

He added 'obsessive chewing' to the list, then pointed to the word *'autistic.'* "Anyone get a better read on this?"

Dr. Phillips shrugged. "The girl *is* non-verbal, and she won't look at anyone straight on. That indicates autism."

"She screamed like a banshee the first time I went near her," Jason added. "Did that happen to anyone else?"

"Maybe she just doesn't like you, Drake. You

know that old wives' tale—children and dogs instinctively know the good guys from the bad guys," Dr. Riser quipped.

Both Phillips and Riser laughed on cue.

Definitely too much group-think. He would need to change a team member soon.

"Actually, she's opposed to all people touching her—except for Dr. Drake, right?" Stephanie said. Was she taking up the case for him, or just pointing out the fallacy in the other doctors' observations?

In answer to her probing look, both Drs. Riser and Phillips nodded affirmation.

Stephanie drummed her fingers on the table. "Being non-verbal is also an indicator of a hearing deficiency. That could explain why she doesn't look at the person speaking. She may be partially deaf and can't figure out where the sound is coming from."

Dr. Phillips smirked. "Dr. Drake checked her hearing and her reflex reaction at the same time."

Stephanie would end up with a wrinkled forehead if she kept frowning like that. "What did you do?"

Dr. Riser answered for him. "Drake sneaked up behind the girl and dropped a food tray. The child jumped and turned around to look in the direction of the noise."

Riser leaned back in his chair. "I thought the mother was going to take a swing at him. You may be a lot of things, Drake, but daddy material isn't one of them. I wouldn't have been surprised if she had lodged a complaint. That's all we need with the lawsuit ongoing right now."

Jason saw a look of pain cross Stephanie's face. Was the department's legal problems causing her that much heartache?

Dr. Phillips nodded. "The lawyers need to settle it soon. The hospital's credibility is suffering."

Jason couldn't help but agree. His own caseload was the lightest he'd seen since he'd been at Sheffield Memorial. Normally he had to turn down more cases than he accepted.

"Not the whole hospital. Just our department," Riser clarified. "I hear you're helping out in the E.R. now, Drake. I could put in a good word for you with one of the specialties, if you want."

Jason brushed off Riser's offer, along with his condescending tone. "No need. I've already turned them all down."

Being certified in pediatrics, internal medicine and surgery, Jason had been asked to assist on every floor of the hospital—by the same staff who registered complaints when he overstepped their bureaucracy to save their patients.

Instead, since his residency in an inner-city free clinic had more than prepared him for the E.R., he'd agreed to help out his friend and department head Dr. Mike Tyler. While the pace was frantic at times, the cases had been fairly routine so far, and once his shift was over he was done. No getting lost in late nights, researching until he was too exhausted to think.

The lack of complex problems to solve made getting over the infant's loss more difficult. His modus operandi was to throw himself into his work. Or, for a while there, into Stephanie's arms.

Now that option was gone, too. Hopefully, like the shortfall of patients, it would be a temporary problem.

It wasn't just the sex.

They fit together mentally as well as physically. They laughed at the same obscure jokes, watched the same TV shows, liked the same food, and best of all they communicated on the same wavelength. Stephanie *got* him. She really got him. And he got her, too.

He'd never experienced that kind of compatibility before. He'd bet a back-rub, followed by a front-rub would fix them both right up without either of them having to say a word between them. If she'd just give their relationship a chance.

Relationship? That was a pretty strong word.

"Let's get back to Maggie."

Relationship. Put *intimate* in front of that and Jason could live with it. In fact he could live with it a lot better than he could live without it.

"Anyone have anything further to add?"

Stephanie shrugged her shoulders, as if shrugging off her worries.

"Macular degeneration," she said. "Have you tested Maggie's sight? Having only peripheral vision would explain the child's lack of eye contact."

"Possible." Jason agreed.

Stephanie was so brilliant. He loved being around her. Love? Another strong word. This time purely used as a figure of speech. Love wasn't in his scope of training.

"I'll order the test. Anything else?"

Dr. Phillips' phone vibrated.

He scowled, letting her know how he felt about the interruption.

She checked the display, then rose. "I can't stay."

Dr. Riser's phone buzzed, too. He grimaced an apology as he glanced at his watch. "An appointment."

At noon? Both of them?

Jason would bet his lunch they'd preplanned this

mutiny so they wouldn't have to skip another noon break.

Yes, he worked his team hard. Anyone who partnered with him needed to show unflagging dedication, and a missed meal on occasion was part of the package.

Riser and Phillips headed for the door.

Stephanie stood, too. But she didn't make a move to leave. "Dr. Drake, could I speak privately with you for a moment?"

Dr. Drake? She only addressed him so formally in front of patients, or on occasion in bed.

"Of course." He closed the door to the conference room.

So she was finally ready to forgive him for missing dinner the weekend before last. It was about time. She'd ignored him for two whole weeks. Though, to be fair, she'd been away for one of them for a directors' conference.

"We both know how quickly rumors spread in this hospital. I need this to be kept confidential between you and me."

Jason's expectations crashed. Stephanie had been worried that their relationship might cause problems with their work. If she suggested they carry on covertly he would refuse. He wouldn't be anyone's dirty little secret.

"Stephanie, we're two consenting adults. What goes on between the two of us—"

"This is strictly business, Dr. Drake." A fleeting expression of something—sorrow?—crossed her eyes before she blinked it away. "We now have an open position in Diagnostics. I would like your opinion on several of our prospects before I contact them for discussion."

She thought about the pulmonary doctor's resignation, locked away in her desk drawer. Now, with Sheffield Memorial's name on the verge of making the gossip rags and tabloids, was not a good time to be enticing new doctors into the hospital. Hopefully Jason's involuntary sacrifice would put a stop to the talk.

But that was a problem for tomorrow.

"Absolutely." Jason's lips twisted into a cynical grimace. "Let's eliminate the candidates that might claim to have sham appointments during consultation meetings first. We've already got two doctors like that."

"Drs. Phillips and Riser's fake pages were rather immature, weren't they? I've talked to both of them about being firm and telling you they aren't at their best when they work through lunch, but they're intimidated by you."

"Intimidated? Why?"

"You're so intense."

"I'm focused."

"Yes, you are." *Too focused—to the exclusion of everything and everyone else.* "No one can refute your dedication to medicine, Dr. Drake."

He used his work as a shield, to keep everyone at a distance. While she had glimpsed the deep sensitivity Jason covered with sarcastic scowls and a cutting wit, she needed more than an occasional lapse in cynicism. She needed a man with a whole heart as well as an exceptional brain and outstanding body.

"*You're* not intimidated by me."

She laughed, but it came out bitter. "Remember who my father is. Dr. William Montclair is known the world over for his intensity of purpose. And my mother isn't a slouch in that department, either."

Jason waved away the mention of the formidable Dr. William Montclair and his spouse, Dr. Clarice Sheffield-Montclair.

"We're good together, Stephanie."

Yes, they were. She could smell his cologne, feel his body heat. His tone made her quiver to the core. Instinctively she felt herself leaning toward him.

She licked her lips.

His eyes followed her movement, like a cat ready to pounce. Intense didn't begin to cover it.

She missed him so desperately, even if he was bad medicine. Being in a room alone with him was not a good thing for her. He was like an addiction. A quick high when they were wrapped arm-in-arm, followed by a debilitating low when he detached and became solitary again.

Which he'd done as soon as she'd tried to take their relationship to a deeper level.

"Jason, I'd prefer to keep things professional at the hospital." Staying firm in her decision to stay apart took all her will-power—especially when he made no secret of the fact he wanted her.

That would end as soon as he found out about the baby.

"And impersonal outside the hospital. I got that from the phone message you left me. Did I say something to offend you?" He looked into her eyes as if he were trying to look into her head—or her heart. Without question, he had immense intensity.

"No, it wasn't anything you said."

While he'd certainly offended everyone else who'd ever walked through the hospital doors, he'd never offended her. He was egotistical, stubborn, overbearing and totally without tact, but she understood him. She could handle all his bad qualities, but she couldn't handle his inability to open himself up to her, his inability to put her first at least on occasion.

"Is this about the missed dinner date? I explained that I needed to read through the lab results so I would know if I needed to order additional tests. Did I do something wrong?" he challenged, certain that another medically related reason would excuse him.

"Other than all those other missed dinner dates and all those refusals to accompany me to social functions? No, you did nothing wrong." Nothing but be himself. But then he'd done nothing right— outside the bedroom.

The night he'd missed their dinner—the dinner during which she had planned to tell him about their baby—had been the breaking point. As she had scraped the congealed gourmet meal into the trash, blown out the candles and exchanged her negligee for her favorite oversized T-shirt and gym shorts, she'd known she couldn't fool herself any longer.

Swathed in her flannel robe, she'd settled in on the couch, hoping. Yet she'd known he wouldn't show. This was how her baby's life would be if she married him. Always waiting for Daddy to come home. She'd lived it with both her parents, feeling guilty all the while for resenting the time they spent with sick children while she'd been well and healthy. And alone.

I'll not do that to you, little one. I'll be here for you, any time you need me.

She wasn't quite sure how she would accomplish that yet, but there had to be a way to balance home life with hospital life.

She took a long look at Jason. He just wasn't the home-and-hearth type. Anything that couldn't be analyzed under a microscope had no place in his life.

Jason raised a sardonic eyebrow. "I really see no reason for you to kick me out of your personal life just because I turned down a gala or two, choosing the art of medicine over the act of socializing. Faux fawning is *not* what I majored in during med school."

He hid his hurt behind his bristling posture.

She had thought they were beyond that. That he had stopped using the mask with her. Maybe they had been before she'd called it quits between them.

"This isn't about the parties."

He'd said more than once that he didn't do emotions, but he'd lied. He'd shown her plenty of passion. And for a while there she had thought he'd also shown her caring and concern and an occasional glimpse of vulnerability. Maybe it had only been in her imagination to start with.

Now it didn't matter. He'd known she'd needed to talk. She'd told him it was important. Standing her up for dinner had been a non-verbal response louder than a shout. She just wasn't enough for him to step outside his comfort zone.

If he wouldn't risk his emotions for her then he wouldn't for his child, either.

"But you just said—" He dropped the attitude. "I don't understand, Stephanie."

This was a huge admission when he prided himself on his intellect. He really *didn't* understand.

"Jason, I want more." She reached out to him, then pulled her hand back before she could make contact. "It's not you. It's me."

Jason rolled his eyes at the platitude.

It *was* her. They'd both agreed from the beginning that neither wanted a serious relationship. Jason would readily admit that his work was his mistress.

She had breached her part of the bargain and taken this much further than an informal friendship with bedroom benefits.

Then, that night at his cabin in the mountains, when they'd lain on his porch looking into the black sky at the pinpoints of stars above, he'd reached for her hand and she'd known. His touch had made more than her skin tingle. It had made her soul vibrate in accord with his. Life and love had flowed through their clasped hands, intertwining their hearts.

That was when she'd known, Jason filled a place inside her that no one else ever could—a place in her heart made just for him from the moment she was born.

Being honest with herself, she'd known their relationship had been destined to become more from the start—at least for her. She didn't do casual sex—and, as guarded as Jason had always been about his dating life, she was sure he didn't either.

But then neither did he do commitment. And raising a child took more commitment than a dozen medical degrees.

Destiny didn't guarantee happily-ever-after, and now she had a child to think about.

That was why she'd had to break it off with him, even though it had broken her heart. *She* might be able to suffer through a casual come-and-go relationship, but she would never subject her child to that kind of pain and uncertainty.

She needed to create a stable environment that would surround and protect her child with love. She was prepared to do that. She had the financial means, the emotional capacity, and by the time her child was born she would have her work-life in perspective, too.

Now was the time. Before she burst into hormonal tears she needed to tell him about the baby and then walk away.

Now. She should tell him now, while she had his undivided attention. "Jason, I need—"

His phone vibrated. He held up a finger to wait.

"Drake here," he answered. Not a word wasted on social niceties. "No, Doctor, I can take your call. We've played tag trying to communicate long enough."

His eyes clouded as he looked through her. Another medical matter taking precedence over her. Was it too much to ask to be first? To know that their child would be first in Jason's life if only for a second?

Yes. It *was* too much to ask. While Jason was devoted to the practice of medicine, extending such devotion to a personal relationship was beyond his capabilities. She had to resign herself to that.

She reached for her lab coat, flailing to find the armhole. He'd been so eager to help her off with it, but he didn't even notice her struggle now.

Nor did he notice when she slipped out, silently shutting the consultation room door behind her.

CHAPTER THREE

JASON kept his hand tightly wrapped around his phone to keep from reaching out and holding Stephanie back—pulling her close to him and never letting her go.

He used all his discipline to concentrate on the question the doctor at the Mayo Clinic was asking. "Dr. Drake, do we have a bad connection?"

"No, I hear you. I'm thinking." He reviewed the question he'd been asked. "Have you considered a gluten sensitivity? They disguise themselves in a multitude of ways, and many of your patient's symptoms match, even though the test results might not indicate a full-blown allergic reaction. I suggest a gluten-free diet for the next fourteen days. Be sure to record behavioral changes as well as antibody levels."

"*I need—*" she'd said. Jason wanted to fulfill that need, whatever it was. But he was pretty sure her need was emotional, and he knew his limitations. He was good at understanding bodies, not emotions. If anyone knew that about him she did. She knew him better than he knew himself most of the time.

How could he give her something he didn't understand?

"I'll give it a try."

Jason was vaguely aware the phone line had gone dead at the other end.

It had begun so simply. A late night of research after the rest of his team had left for their family obligations.

Stephanie had gotten comfortable, kicked off her shoes and replaced her contacts with glasses.

Then she'd noticed his stiff neck, from hours spent hunched over the computer terminal, and offered to massage the ache away.

But the massage had backfired. Instead of relieving his tension, her hands had set him on fire.

Unable to concentrate on the case any longer, they'd called it a night.

But fate had intervened. In the parking lot she'd pulled up next to his motorcycle as he'd been about to strap on his helmet. The light mist of early evening had been turning into a heavy drizzle.

"Want a ride?" she asked.

"Sure." He thought—hoped—she offered more than transportation, but he wasn't sure until he climbed into her red low-slung sports car and she gave him the choice. "My place or yours?"

The whole moment felt like a clichéd scene from a nineteen-fifties *film noir*, but it was effective nonetheless.

Stephanie cooked a meal—of sorts. She shoved a frozen foil tray of lasagna into the oven, set the temperature, and handed him a bottle of Chianti and a corkscrew.

After popping the cork, he stripped off Stephanie's high heels, one by one, letting his fingers do a slow examination from her toes to the arches of her feet to her very sensitive ankles. As he ran his thumb along the arch of her foot, she moaned and arched her back, emphasizing the peaks of her magnificent breasts.

He explored the erogenous and sensitive ankle-bone, circling his finger until her breath came in short wisps. Her passion brought out the hero in him. He wanted to find a dragon to slay to keep her eyes shining in admiration.

Her hands fluttered to his chest and along his shoulders. A low, deep growl started deep inside him as his hunger for her built.

Her usually graceful fingers fumbled at the edge of her sweater as she tried to pull if off. He helped, covering her hands with his own. His own breath caught as he revealed her silky skin hidden underneath.

As if she were shy, she held back as long as she could, but by the time he reached the band of her thong she was ripping off his shirt and tugging at his belt.

They'd ended up overcooking the lasagna and washing it down with too much wine. And he'd never slept so peacefully as that night in her arms.

He and Stephanie had been of one mind: they were the perfect high-stress couple. They enjoyed each other's company, enjoyed the mutual benefits of an exciting sex-life and understood neither of them had room for more than a series of one-night stands.

That had been at first, but he'd soon figured out that Stephanie wasn't the kind of woman that a man could treat casually. He'd tried his best to treat her as well as she deserved. She was a prize, a hidden treasure.

And he'd prized knowing that she wore a kinky thong under her skirts and tailored trousers. He'd prized even more the fact that he was the only one who knew.

Or at least he *had* been the only one.

Obviously his best hadn't been good enough.

Who was that soft glow for? Was she dating someone already?

No. As fast as word traveled throughout the hospital, he would have heard. Wouldn't he?

And why was he still dwelling on it? He'd broken off relationships before, quickly and cleanly with no regrets.

That their break-up bothered him at all was a clue that their relationship had mutated into more than he had intended. He probably would have insisted they take a step or two backward himself if she hadn't called it off between them. Probably.

But a total severance of the relationship was a bit extreme.

Stephanie didn't need to amputate the head to cure the headache, did she? What was wrong with the "two aspirin and call me in the morning" approach?

He knew she'd been under severe pressure ever since their department had been hit with the big lawsuit. He could understand how she could be overwhelmed. But lawsuits settled down eventually. She would come back to him in due course if only he could find the patience to wait. Right?

And she was definitely worth the wait.

Until then he would bury himself in his work.

He smiled in anticipation as he cranked up his

music. Pulling up a half-dozen resources on his computer screen, he reviewed Maggie's list of symptoms.

Exhilaration coursed through his veins as he lost himself in the hunt for the elusive answer. Yes, unraveling the mysteries of medicine was what he'd been born for.

Everything else was secondary.

Why, then, did memories of Stephanie naked in his bed keep distracting him from his purpose in life?

Once safely behind her office door, Stephanie let her shoulders sag. That was twice she'd tried to tell him about the baby and twice he'd let duty distract him.

Maybe she should send him a text message.

Or maybe she should say nothing at all. He'd notice soon enough anyway.

He was one of the topmost recognized diagnosticians in the country. She was surprised he hadn't already guessed. Maybe he didn't want to know.

If he asked, she'd tell the truth. Otherwise it wasn't as if she wanted or needed anything from him. She had the monetary capacity to take care of her child herself. And she was determined to have the nurturing capacity, too. Unlike Jason Drake.

After her rallying self-talk she expected to feel strong. Instead she just felt lonely.

She pushed the button on the intercom. "Marcy, has my dress been delivered yet?"

"Yes, I'll bring it in."

"Thanks."

Marcy gave a perfunctory knock on the door before coming in, carrying the dress covered by a garment bag. "The seamstress sends apologies but she wasn't able to let the dress out at all."

"I was worried about that. I'll just have to wear it as is." She should have checked her wardrobe sooner, but hadn't realized how much her body was changing until last night, when trying on her formal wear.

"Could I see it?" asked Marcy.

"Sure." Stephanie unzipped the bag.

Cocktail-length, red, sequined, halter-topped and backless. She'd originally bought the dress for an Independence Day gala. Now it was the only one that still fit her swollen breasts. It stretched much tighter across her torso and her derriere, too, giving her a vintage Marilyn Monroe look that she'd never had before.

"Wow! That will make a statement."

Since the dress was so much glitzier than the pale, elegant chiffons she usually wore, it was sure to raise eyebrows among those who knew her. Being dateless, she would have to stand up to the scrutiny all by herself—a test of her self-confidence and poise.

She might as well get used to her single state. She would *not* be dating *anyone* for a long while.

She did *not* need another complication in her life, and she'd never been the kind of woman who had to appear on a man's arm to make herself feel confident.

Although she had to admit she'd had her fantasies about Jason Drake.

"I bought it two months ago for the big Independence Day celebration and ended up not going. But tonight, with our supermodel and her friends in attendance, I thought it might be appropriate."

When Stephanie had originally tried it on she'd indulged in a bit of daydreaming, imagining the look of desire in Jason's eyes as she took off her evening stole.

She had intended to invite him to a white tie evening of fine dining, a full-scale orchestra and fireworks viewed from the rooftop of a prominent hotel to celebrate Independence Day.

Of course imagining Jason even accompanying her had been a fantasy. Every formal function she'd asked him to attend he'd cancelled on her, or flat-out turned her down.

"Dr. Drake is going to drag you back to his cave when he sees you in this," Marcy said.

"Why would you think I was going with Dr. Drake?"

Marcy looked puzzled, then embarrassed. "I thought that break-up thing was just a rumor to throw off everyone at the hospital. He bought a ticket at the head table next to you as soon as I put out the invitation list two weeks ago."

"He did?" Stephanie couldn't imagine why. "Marcy, are you sure? Attending galas and balls is not on Dr. Drake's list of favorite pastimes. He's probably never put on a tux in his life."

"Not that he needs one." Marcy grinned. "Scrubs suit him just fine."

Yes, they did. More than that, they defined him. He was a medical professional inside and out. She should know. She'd seen him both ways.

Stephanie turned away to hide her reaction to memories of Jason both in and out of his scrubs.

"Thanks, Marcy, for bringing in my dress." As she rezipped the garment bag she couldn't stop herself from imagining how Jason's hand on her back would feel as he unzipped the dress for her.

What would he look like in a tux, tie hanging loose around his neck, pearl buttons undone enough to show the firmness of his well-defined pecs?

Of course she would enjoy removing *any* type of clothing he wore. She had loved peeling off his scrub shirt that first time.

And the feel of his well-washed T-shirt, still warm from his body, wrapped around her own body… It gave her quivers just thinking about it.

Jason wore casual clothes with the charismatic attitude of the ultimate bad boy. The aged jeans and T-shirts he wore after work and on weekends molded to his rebellious personality as well as his athletic shape.

All those hours he spent scaling mountains and fighting white-water rapids made for sure-footed grace and iron-hard muscles.

In a moment of passion, she'd asked to go with him one weekend. When he suggested an Independence Day campout instead of the gala she'd traded in high heels for hiking boots, eaten charbroiled burgers to the music of night birds, then watched the stars pop against a velvet sky. She'd never seen anything so spectacular.

That was the weekend the baby had been conceived.

With great self-control, Stephanie turned her thoughts from fantasy to reality.

There would be no happy little traditional family for her child. But Stephanie knew from first-hand experience that the traditional two-parent family didn't automatically equal a happy childhood. Not when the parents couldn't find time for their child.

Without thinking, her hand drifted to her round belly. Her child would never suffer for lack of parental attention. She would make sure of it.

After an hour of distraction when he should have been researching, Jason headed downstairs to the E.R. for some advice. His friend Mike had had a similar dilemma only a year ago. Apparently he'd figured things out, since he was now married with a new baby.

He and Mike Tyler had been roommates after Mike had answered his ad for a roommate to share expenses during pre-med. Although neither of them were big conversationalists, after years of rooming, which had lasted through pre-med, medical school and residency, Mike was the closest friend Jason had. Mike had introduced Jason to hiking and rafting all those years ago, giving him an effective outlet for letting off steam and finding an occasional glimpse of inner peace.

Now Mike worked the E.R. at Sheffield Memorial, thriving on the excitement, while Jason preferred the details and intrigue of diagnostics and research.

Both he and Mike had come a long way since they'd had to share one winter coat between the two of them in their younger days.

Last year Mike had married into an instant family of two girls and a boy, along with a beautiful, witty wife who'd just given birth to their son eight weeks ago.

Somehow Mike made it work.

Jason waited while Mike examined a chef's gashed forefinger and ordered a tetanus shot along with a couple of stitches.

When Mike was finally free, Jason asked, "You up for a hike this weekend? I've got some relationship questions to ask you."

A good, hard climb in the crisp mountain air would clear his head.

"Can't. I've got to take the five-year-old to a birthday party. Tea party theme. The birthday girl's father has promised grown-up drinks for the parents while we wait." He sighed, but his eyes sparkled with happiness. "The sacrifices of fatherhood."

Jason couldn't imagine himself at a little girl's

birthday party, making small talk with other parents. Even the thought of being so domestically entrapped made him fidget.

"We've got the waiting room cleared out. Ask me now."

Jason shifted from foot to foot, then just blurted it out. "When a woman says she needs more, what does she mean?"

"More, huh? That's a tricky one." Mike rubbed his chin. "Are we talking about Dr. Montclair?"

Jason chose to ignore the smirk Mike didn't bother to hide. "Yes. Who else would it be?"

"She strikes me as a straightforward woman. Why don't you ask her for specifics?"

Jason thought that one over. By his evaluation, their latest conversation hadn't been too straightforward.

"You're not much help."

"Guys generally aren't when it comes to women. Why don't you come by the house on Sunday and ask Caroline? She's good at this sort of thing."

"Caroline doesn't like me."

"She's forgiven you." Mike clapped him on the shoulder. "Never tell a pregnant woman she should cut back on the chocolate, even if she should. The closer they get to their due dates, the testier they get."

"Lesson learned."

A nurse peeked into the lounge. "Dr. Tyler, we've got a patient for you."

Jason took the stairs two at a time, but the dank, enclosed staircase didn't give him what he needed.

He needed to work off some excess energy in the fresh air and sunshine. Wide open spaces normally cleared his cramped brain.

For safety reasons Jason never hiked alone. But he was tempted to risk it. That was what women did—made men do foolish things.

No, he wouldn't risk going it alone with no one to call on for help. No woman was worth being stuck stranded on a mountain with a broken leg. *Or a broken heart.*

No. Not a broken heart. He would have to love Stephanie for that to happen, and he'd promised long ago to never be that foolish again.

Stephanie's phone rang, showing Jason's office number. He never called. He was a face-to-face kind of guy. Warily, she picked it up. "Hello?"

"Stephanie, when you said you needed…" He paused, giving Stephanie time to catch up with his one-sided conversation. "What is it you need?"

What should she answer? *I need you to show me your heart? I need you to love me? I need you to put me first in your life?* "I need you to attend a sensitivity training class."

"A what?"

"A sensitivity class."

"Why?"

"You've got another complaint filed against you, I'm afraid." Yes, that sounded nice and business-like. Stephanie was rather proud of her control.

"So?"

"So the hospital is being very careful about these things nowadays, particularly because of the law-suit. The class is mandatory."

"Or what? You'll fire me?"

At the thought of never seeing Jason again Stephanie felt her stomach drop. "No, Jason. Of course not—not you, anyway. But showing that we insist upon a consistent policy will help with the lawsuit and our malpractice insurance. I need you to cooperate with me."

"What's the complaint?"

"Mrs. Canover said you were rude to her."

"Remembering Mrs. Canover, I would have to agree with her."

"Jason, we've discussed this before. A large part of patient care is attitude. We treat the whole pa-tient and the family, not just the illness."

"No, that's not in my job description. My job is

to find the problem and fix it. Has Mrs. Canover's son had a relapse? Difficulty breathing? Rash? Fever? Sore throat?"

"No. None of that. Her son is recovering nicely."

"Then what's her complaint?"

"Did you really tell her she should stick with growing African Violets instead of children?"

"The woman demanded that I give her three-year-old son allergy shots twice a week rather than getting rid of her houseplants. What would *you* have said?" Jason had been staggered when the woman had refused to give up the prize-winning African Violets that had been passed down through generations for the health of her son, and hadn't hesitated to give his opinion.

Frankly, Stephanie agreed. But, as her grandmother insisted, there was a polite way to say everything. "I'm not sure, but I probably wouldn't have implied she was as dumb as the dirt in her violet pots."

"Who will take care of my patients while I'm stuck in a classroom being lectured to by an idiot who has never diagnosed an illness in his life?"

"You will. I've scheduled the class for your off hours this weekend."

"I've already got plans."

An unexpected spike of jealousy shot through

Stephanie. The thought of Jason with another woman sent her temples to pounding.

Not good for the baby, she reminded herself. She took a deep breath. "Cancel them. I'm sure your date will understand. After all, you're a doctor. Any woman who makes plans with you should expect to be flexible."

"Just because we agreed to see other people doesn't mean I am." He lowered his voice a half-octave, probably because he knew how she liked that. "I was hoping you might want to get away this weekend. We could go to my cabin. We haven't been up there since Independence Day. I could make lasagna."

"Our personal relationship is over, remember?"

"Stephanie, just because our sexual liaison is over it doesn't mean—" He swallowed hard enough for her to hear him. "Doesn't mean we can't still be friends."

His voice sounded strained. As honest and forthright as he was, he wasn't good at voicing what others wanted to hear.

She narrowed her eyes. "You're just saying that to get me back into your bed, aren't you?"

"Busted." He sounded awkward, sheepish. "You've got to admit we're awesome together."

She looked up, as if searching for an answer in the ceiling tiles. "Jason—"

"I know you have a lot going right now, Stephanie. We could both use a little fun to put things into perspective." He sounded serious. "No strings. No commitments. Just a weekend away. A glass of wine under the stars and a few laughs between friends."

That had been more than enough for her only a few short months ago.

They had shared some fun times. His quirky sense of humor was right in line with hers. Together they had snickered and chortled at things the rest of the world didn't get. It had felt good to be understood.

"There's more to life than grins and giggles, Jason."

She took off her glasses to wipe her eyes with the back of her hand. "I'll email you the details on the class."

Stephanie spent the rest of the afternoon familiarizing herself with Jason's patient files, all the while marveling at his brilliance. His reports made for fascinating reading. They were thorough and detailed—and, best of all, unbiased. He didn't slant the facts to support his hypotheses, and he included details of wrong assumptions as readily as right ones.

While all doctors were supposed to be this objective, Stephanie had never found one whose ego didn't shade the facts at least a little bit until Jason.

Lost in work, she didn't realize the time until Marcy buzzed her over the intercom. "Just letting you know I'm leaving for the day. Should I bring in your messages?"

"Yes, please." Stephanie glanced at her watch. Where had the time gone?

Marcy brought in a fistful of messages and notes to be returned and laid them in the in-box on Stephanie's desk.

Stephanie gave them a casual glance. "Anything urgent?"

"Just the usual. Dr. Sim in Obstetrics wants you to set up an appointment with her. She didn't mention the topic of discussion. Do I need to get information on the meeting agenda?"

"No, Dr. Sim and I have talked previously." Soon everyone would know why she had appointments with the obstetrician. But not tonight. Tonight her baby was still her little secret.

Stephanie folded that particular note and slipped it into her lab coat's pocket. "Anything else?"

"Another in-house complaint against Dr. Drake."

"Can it wait until tomorrow?"

"Yes, I'm sure it can. And your mother's personal assistant called. Should she send the car here for you tonight?"

Stephanie thought of answering no, saying she would drive herself. But she suddenly drooped with exhaustion—mentally as well as physically. She didn't know how late it would be before she could gracefully exit the Baby Isaac Benefit.

While she had intended to run home to do make-up and hair, the drive would steal minutes from her day. She could pin her ponytail into a ballerina bun, and she had sufficient cosmetics to do an acceptable make-up job here at the office. That way she could squeeze in a much-needed rest first.

While she didn't have a lot of time for a nap, she didn't need a lot. Just a few minutes to prop up her feet and close her eyes.

As a resident, she had perfected the art of napping. Fifteen minutes had always been enough to restore her flagging energy and weary mind.

"Tell her yes. I would appreciate having the car sent here. And keep my office phone on hold."

As soon as Marcy left Stephanie dimmed the lights, kicked off her shoes and settled onto her couch.

When she heard the *bing* from her computer

that let her know she'd received an email, she ignored it. Unlike her parents and her ex-lover, she knew how to manage her priorities, and right now a quick nap was at the top of her list.

Only six o'clock and she felt as if she could sleep through to the morning. Too many late nights, early mornings, and busy days in between were taking their toll. She needed to take a long look at her schedule and eliminate non-essential functions for the next several months. Possibly longer. It was time to take care of herself.

At least for fifteen minutes.

Just as she was drifting off to sleep, her office door burst open, slamming back on its hinges.

"When were you going to tell me?" Jason demanded, more emotion in his face than she had ever seen. Unfortunately that emotion was anger—at her.

Sitting up too quickly made her light-headed. She blinked through the spots as she tried to gather her thoughts.

Caught off-guard, she thought fast before leading with her most calming reassurance. "I'll take care of everything. There's nothing you need to do."

He waved a computer printout in front of her.

"You've already done enough, don't you think? How much was my reputation worth?"

"What?" Stephanie scrunched her toes, feeling vulnerable in her bare feet. Reaching up from the couch, she grabbed the emailed page from his hand and scanned enough to see the hospital's law firm was informing all named parties of their agreement. "Oh."

"Oh?" He grabbed the back of a chair, his knuckles white. "Do you believe I did anything negligent to cause that baby's death?"

"No. Of course not."

Was that relief she saw in his eyes as they settled into a less turbulent gray?

"Then why, Stephanie? Why make *me* the scapegoat?"

"To protect the hospital." She stood, feeling vulnerable again with him standing over her as she sat on the couch. Still, shoeless, her standing didn't make much difference. "Sheffield Memorial would have been gravely injured in the media circus they were threatening. Our lawyers felt that even if we won the lawsuit—which was unlikely—we would still lose in public opinion, which means funding and research grants and patients. We've already seen some of that come true. Instead Isaac's parents settled for an internal investigation, with the doctor responsible for Isaac's death being officially sanctioned."

"Sanctioned? How so?"

"I oversee all your cases personally."

"I've got a standing invitation to join the Mayo Clinic. Maybe it's time I accepted their offer."

"Why haven't you already?"

Wasn't that what she wanted? Jason out of her life?

"I thought I had everything I wanted here."

Did that mean her? Or only Sheffield Memorial.

Sheffield needed him. It was her duty to try to keep him.

What about the baby? She pushed away that intrusive thought. She would never use her child to bind Jason in any way.

"It's only for a while. Six months or so." She tried to placate him. Then she would be on maternity leave and someone else would supervise his work for the next six months. But she would save that for later.

"Anything else? Does this settlement come with other repercussions you haven't seen fit to reveal to me? Or should I wait for the email?"

"We've agreed to invest a significant amount of money into neonatal improvements." She gestured to her dress on the coat rack. "My parents are holding a fundraiser tonight for the Baby Isaac Commemorative Endowment Fund."

"But this party has been planned for weeks."

"Yes, this is the annual Sheffield-Montclair hospital fundraiser, with a twist. During the first round of negotiations my father and mother readily agreed to donate the proceeds to kick off the endowment."

"Then what took so long to settle?"

"I had to do a lot of soul-searching to give you up as a sacrifice."

"Good to know I wasn't just a casual snap of the fingers. But the end result is the same, isn't it?" He turned from her to look out her window. "My reputation is sullied and I work under your orders."

"I had to. For the sake of the hospital." Her decision had seemed the only right one to make at the time. Why was she now sure she had committed a major mistake? Although she could still think of no better way. "I'm sorry I've hurt you."

"*Hurt* me? I've always known where I stood with you, Stephanie." He pinned her with a hard, cold stare. "You've only proved me right where I wished I was wrong."

He left as abruptly as he had come.

Stephanie had wanted more emotion from him. She had gotten what she wished for.

Now she feared she would have a difficult time living with the flood of disappointment and pain he'd shown her.

Jason strapped on his helmet, fastened his leather jacket and straddled his motorcycle. As he wove in and out of traffic for the freedom of the highway he laughed at his own arrogance. He'd thought he'd meant more to her than that.

She'd meant more to him.

Wait. She'd meant—*what* to him?

He didn't want to think about it. Not now. Not ever.

He had the strongest urge to ride to his cabin in the mountains, his retreat from the world. Safety partner or not, he would run the footpaths until he was exhausted, then drop into bed, too tired to think. But the five-hour round trip wasn't practical when he wanted to be back in his office early tomorrow to check Maggie's latest test results.

Instead he settled for exchanging scrubs for running shoes and attempted to sweat out his angst with a good run around his neighborhood.

As he pounded the pavement he let his thoughts freefall.

He was a good doctor—one of the best.

Yes, he had the highest mortality rate at Sheffield

Memorial. But everyone from the hospital board down to the janitors understood why. He was the doctor of last resort. Too often, when all else failed, the patient was sent to Dr. Drake.

The challenge invigorated him. The frustration he could deal with.

This wasn't the first time he'd been named in a lawsuit and it wouldn't be the last. Only in the past the hospital had fought for him, defended him, believed in him.

Stephanie had believed in him.

She said she still did. Even so she'd betrayed him—sold his reputation to keep Sheffield Memorial's name squeaky-clean.

But the practice wasn't uncommon. This was one of the many reasons why malpractice insurance was so high—and the hospital paid his insurance premiums

So, was it Stephanie's divided loyalties and betrayal, or was it his own ego that had him so angry?

The hospital was her great-grandparents' legacy—a trust passed from generation to generation. With Stephanie being the last of the line, she'd been raised with the duty to keep Sheffield Memorial alive. Some day she would take her father's place as president of the board. Family reputation coupled with career ambitions ran much deeper than loyalty to nonchalantly discarded lovers.

He had to admit Stephanie had been a distraction to his work. Maybe he should thank her for reminding him what was important—saving lives.

Maybe in a hundred years he'd be able to.

His mind drifted to the open invitation he had to join the ranks of doctors at the Mayo Clinic.

Why had he stayed at Sheffield Memorial?

The answer was there in his head, too loud to ignore. Stephanie. He was fascinated by her. *Had been* fascinated by her.

Could he continue to work for her?

He wasn't sure. He didn't think so.

Could he leave and never see her again?

Same answers.

He slowed to a walk as he headed up the steps into his duplex. A quick shower and a call for takeout, then maybe he'd finish that spy thriller novel he'd started reading last night.

But he wasn't in the mood for pizza or Chinese, or any other food in a box that could be delivered to his door.

Hell, what was he doing? Last month he'd paid over fifteen hundred dollars to sit at the Montclairs' table and eat their lobster and steak.

Jason reached for the tuxedo he'd had tailored for the occasion. He was going to get his money's worth tonight—if not in food, then in squirm factor.

CHAPTER FOUR

STEPHANIE crowded Dr. Wilkins behind a potted palm. Her height and her heels gave her the advantage of towering over him. Good for intimidation—except that now his nose was aligned with her cleavage...a cleavage that was much more ample than it had ever been before.

She refused to hunch. Instead she deliberately pulled her shoulders into military straightness. The man was a doctor. He'd seen breasts before.

"An email? You sent him an *email*?" She fought hard to keep her voice to a whisper. Yes, this would be better done in the privacy of an office, but she couldn't wait that long to vent her anger. "I didn't even know it was official yet. What happened to common courtesy? A little warning so I would have time to break the news in person?"

"I tried to call, but your assistant said you didn't want to be bothered."

"So you had to rush out and send an email to everyone and his brother?"

"With the celebrity couple attending tonight, I thought it would be better to let them know ahead of time that we'd made progress."

"Better? Or easier on you?" She pointed her celery stick at him. "Does it feel any easier to you now? What about Dr. Drake? Did you stop and think how *he* might feel?"

"Drake? Feel?" Wilkins dared to grin.

Stephanie used all her will-power to keep herself from wiping that grin off his face.

"If it bothers him that much, we can throw some money at it." Wilkins smiled. "Money fixes most of the world's problems."

Stephanie glanced across the room to the supermodel and her producer husband, huddled together, strain showing on their faces. "I doubt our celebrity couple would agree."

And neither would Jason Drake. She took a deep breath, trying to get her emotions under control.

Was that a licentious smirk on Wilkins's face? Did the man know she had eyes in addition to breasts? He was old enough to be her father, for heaven's sake.

She shook the celery stick at him again. "Never let it be said that I discourage monetary compensation for my staff. By all means have the board give Jason a raise if that soothes their consciences about what we've done. May I suggest thirty pieces of silver as recompense?"

The room fell silent around her. Had she shouted when she had intended to whisper? Or was it one of those odd moments that occurred naturally at large affairs.

She looked around and saw everyone's attention drawn to the entrance stairs.

Dr. Jason Drake.

Could this day get any worse?

Jason stood on the top step at the entrance to the banquet hall, looking down at all the elegant people milling around on the marble ballroom floor below. The way the room was designed, he might have been stepping into Cinderella's ballroom scene.

The politely hushed conversation sounded like a political rally on mute, underscored by chamber music. Which, when he thought about it, was exactly what this gala was.

The wealthiest couples in the city had come tonight to help out the Montclair-Sheffield family. Politicians, business-owners, doctors from all over the city—all with their spouses either at their elbows or working the room nearby.

The room was languidly awhirl with black tuxedoes identical to the one he wore and conservatively tasteful pastel evening gowns. He caught an occasional glimpse of a trophy wife's enhanced cleavage visible through the glitter of diamonds hung around her neck.

A sprinkling of B-list celebrities dotted the crowd, identifiable by their flashier colors, gaudy faux jewelry and short bursts of loud laughter— all designed to draw the attention of any attending media.

"Dr. Jason Drake," the major-domo bellowed, breaking through the sibilant conversation.

Everyone turned toward the entrance, assessing and judging him.

A gaggle of the hospital's lawyers stood near a brightly-lit potted plant as if they were eavesdropping on it. They stared at him while they whispered behind their drink-filled hands.

The stares were quickly averted, but he still caught expressions of disbelief and, in general, unwelcome.

Maybe he should have settled for take-out instead.

Instead he stood taller, lifted his chin and dared anyone to question his presence. He had a very expensive gala ticket in his pocket, should anyone confront him. He'd paid for the right to attend just like everyone else.

He recognized several doctors and a scattering of board members. One of them raised his glass in salute.

Jason acknowledged it with a slight nod.

From his vantage point he scanned the room, looking for the open bar. He would *not* look for Stephanie tonight. He didn't need her to smooth his way. He was Dr. Jason Drake, a brilliant doctor in his own right.

Still, a bright sparkling ruby caught his eye in the midst of all the wilting pastel flowers.

Stephanie. Even though she was turned away from him he recognized her.

Her dress had no back. He could imagine tracing his fingers down her spine, hearing her moan for him. Feeling her own fingers tickle across his chest, hearing her whisper in his ear for more. She would smell of meadows and waterfalls and that special scent that was all her own.

And she would transport him to a bliss he'd known only in her arms.

Before he could stop himself, he found his feet moving in her direction. Standing next to her, Wilkins broke off their conversation and grimaced in his direction.

Stephanie turned, shock on her face.

Jason had the presence of mind to give her an expressionless nod before walking past her to the bar.

"What will you have, sir?" The bartender stood ready to serve, the only person in the room who wasn't sending stunned looks his way.

Jason had bartended plenty while working his way through school, but never at a private party. No tip jar. He slipped the boy a twenty.

"Whiskey." He rarely drank. To drink was to give up a modicum of control. In fact he would probably hold this single glass without even sipping until they were called in to dinner. But he liked the smell and the color. Most importantly, the glass gave him a distraction and kept his hands occupied.

"Straight, sir?"

"Sure. Why not?"

Dr. William Montclair approached, and Jason stuck his hand in his pocket to pull out his ticket.

Before he could do so Montclair put his hand on Jason's shoulder, clamping down firmly. Jason took a step away, breaking the connection and tamping down his old fight-or-flight instinct. Taking a swing at a distinguished fellow doctor, the host of the party, would do a lot to deteriorate the respect the lawsuit settlement had already tried to erode.

"I want to personally thank you, Jason, for taking one for the team." If William Montclair noticed Jason's shocked surprise, he overlooked it. "We all know you're one of the best—not just here in Denver, but worldwide—and we're lucky to have you at Sheffield Memorial. The board is grateful to you for submitting to such poor treatment—from us and from them." He nodded toward the lawyers who were now ogling a twenty-something starlet who had just appeared upon the entrance stairs.

"Dr. Montclair—"

"William. Please, call me William." Montclair handed his empty class to the bartender for a refill. "I also want to thank you as a father. You've made this whole ordeal smoother for my daughter. For that you will always have my undying gratitude and respect. You're a good man, Jason. Just treat her gently, won't you, son?"

He shouldn't need it. He was a grown man, a successful doctor. But the validation and the compliments filled an empty place deep inside him.

Jason felt like a sponge in the desert after rainfall at being called anyone's son, even if it was only an expression. But he couldn't claim it.

"About Stephanie and me—we're not—"

Montclair looked past Jason's shoulder. "I see

someone else intent on speaking to you. If you'll excuse me…"

The hairs on the back of Jason's neck prickled before she glided into his peripheral vision.

Then she was next to him.

He breathed her in like a man too long without oxygen.

"Jason. You came."

Did she sound displeased, or simply surprised?

"Could we talk?" She put her hand on his arm to guide him away.

He thought about resisting, finding an excuse to avoid the talk. He didn't need to discuss his inadequacies in relationships again, but evidently she did. According to Mike, women had a need for closure. Jason had always thought they just needed to have the last word.

Either way, if Stephanie needed to talk that much he would suffer through it. Maybe she'd even changed her mind about ending their love-life. *And maybe pigs would fly.*

He studied the worried strain in her eyes.

"Please, Jason."

He couldn't resist. He followed her into the curtained-off alcove where the band would play after dinner.

Following her had advantages. He didn't know

what kind of underwear she could possibly wear under that dress, but the style was certainly making the most of her assets. He would love to ease that zipper down and see. He clenched his fist to keep from reaching out to touch her.

She stopped in the middle of the band's dais. "Why did you come?" Her question caught him by surprise.

"I caught a glimpse of that dress and wanted to see more."

"You didn't seem to care when you saw me earlier."

"I was angry."

"And you're not anymore?"

"Not so much angry as turned on." He went with his impulse and ran his fingertips from her shoulder to her elbow.

He was rewarded when her eyes grew large and dark at his touch.

She took a step back and rubbed her arm, as if to rub off his touch. "You shouldn't be here."

"After all these months trying to get me to attend one of these things with you that's the attitude you take?"

"You didn't attend with me, Jason. You came on your own."

"Did you come with someone else?"

"That's not your concern."

He grinned, hearing her answer in her tone of voice. "You came solo, too." To keep from touching her again, he twirled his whiskey glass in both hands.

"What part of taking a break from our relationship don't you understand, Jason?"

"The part where you forgot to tell me you're pregnant."

The words were out before even he realized what he was saying. Although why it had taken him so long to recognize, he had no idea. Denial, maybe?

For a moment the world stopped turning. Stephanie froze as still as if she were encased in ice. The loudest sound Jason could hear was his own heartbeat in his ears.

Then Stephanie stood straighter, but redirected her glare from his eyes to his shoulder. "Why do you think I'm pregnant?"

He couldn't hold back his snort any better than he had held back his spontaneous diagnosis. "I don't have to be a doctor to read the signs." He leaned forward, studying her closely. "Your breasts are larger, much larger. Round and full. Do they ache?"

"Why, you—why—that's none of your business."

He gave her a wan smile. "How long?"

Her shoulders fell. "You should know. You were there. 'A little condom slippage,' you said. Not a big deal. 'It probably won't matter,' you said. Well, it mattered."

"Abstinence is the only infallible method of birth control."

"That or a well-placed snip." She scissored her fingers at him with such enthusiasm he couldn't keep from wincing.

"Remind me to hide all the scalpels from you."

"You've got to sleep some time."

He set his whiskey glass down on the harpist's chair before he drained it. He needed all his wits around Stephanie right now.

She began to pace, her high heels clicking on the dais floor. The slit up the back of her dress revealed quite a bit of her incredibly long thighs.

He hated to say it, but as a doctor it was his duty. "You should probably start wearing flats. Heels put too much pressure on the spine as the fetus grows."

She stopped right in front of him, inches from his chest. "It's not a fetus. It's a baby."

"Actually—"

"For once, can you drop the medical jargon and be human? It's a little boy or girl—a child—not just a clump of cells that decided to start multiplying when your sperm ran into my ovum." She dared him to negate her. "Baby. Say it. *Baby.*"

He might be insensitive, but he wasn't stupid. He said it. "Baby."

She whirled around, took a step away, then stopped, putting the microphone stand between them. Should he go to her? Stay still? Come back later?

He cleared his throat and offered, "If you want to do it this weekend, I'm free."

"*Do it*, Jason? I have proof that we've already *done it.*" Stephanie pointed to her stomach, which definitely had a bit more fullness to it. That was one of the things he admired about her. She had curves, not just bones and angles.

"No, not that kind of *do it*—although I'm not averse." He leered at her before he got serious again. "I meant discuss the baby. Make plans. We could go up to my cabin, open a bottle of—" no, wine was not on the pregnancy diet "—milk and look at the stars." So much change to take in.

"I am not going anywhere with you. We broke up, remember? There is no need to change that." Her color was more blotchy red right now than glowing.

"No, *you* broke up. I was fine with our relationship."

"Just friends. We were just convenient friends. Isn't that all you wanted to be, Jason?"

"Now we're obviously more." He gestured to her stomach. "We're good together, Stephanie. We need to work this out."

"I tried, remember?" She gave him a bittersweet smile. "It's too little, too late, Jason."

"Because I missed a dinner date with you?"

"Because you missed *many* dinner dates and gala events and movies and simple suppers and cuddle time on the couch in front of the TV, and all the other things we'd planned while we dated. The only thing you never missed was an opportunity to share my bed." Her eyes reflected anger as well as hurt. "I can't be with you because I can't count on you."

"I'm a doctor, Stephanie. You know what that means. Not only are you a doctor yourself, you grew up with doctors for parents. Patients don't get ill only during business hours."

"Yes, I know the drill. Patients always come first." Her eyes glittered with tears. "You're right. I've lived with that all my life. One of my earliest memories was my first day of school. Mom and Dad and I were all going to eat breakfast together, then they would both drive me to kindergarten. We were all going shopping together for my first backpack, my first lunchbox, and a notebook with my favorite cartoon character on the front." She swiped her dry cheek with the back of her hand. "Do you want to know what happened?"

Jason could guess.

Stephanie confirmed it when she said, "First Mom's beeper went off. Then Dad's. Patients. I knew even then that some person needed them more than I did, and that I was being terribly self-ish for resenting that."

Although her eyes brimmed, Stephanie didn't cry. Jason had never seen her cry.

"Then there was my ballet recital, and my first date, and my high school graduation. Even if they did come, I lived in fear of one or the other walking out in the middle, just when I needed them there the most, to go and be hero to some stranger who needed them more. There's always someone…."

He retrieved his glass and took a sip of the potent whiskey so he didn't have to look at the accusation in her eyes. Finally he said what was on the tip of his tongue. "But that's what doctors do. That's who we are."

"Does that mean we can't be more?"

"More?" Jason felt a pang. He still didn't know what *more* was. He walked toward her even though she took two steps back. Only the cello on the stand at her back kept her from putting more distance between them. "Stephanie," he forced out, soft and low. "I know the pain of growing up without a father. I won't doom my child to that same fate."

Stephanie drew back as if she'd just been slapped. "But you'd let your child go through life feeling second-best?"

Jason didn't know how to respond. He felt so helpless. Stephanie's anguish cut him deeply, but emotional pain wasn't his area of expertise. He didn't know how to fix this. He knew of no pill nor procedure to make the pain go away—neither for her nor him.

Still, he couldn't look away. Couldn't dismiss all that raw emotion she'd let him see. Couldn't keep from racking his brain, trying to think of what he could do to make this all better.

He had nothing.

Stephanie broke eye contact first, looking beyond him. Her face cleared of all expression. "Jason, you should go."

Behind him, a shrill, theatrical voice said, "You—"

He whipped around to come face-to-face with the supermodel who was responsible for tonight's whole shindig.

Her silver-sequined dress hung on her skeletal frame. She'd already shed the little baby fat she'd put on, regaining the gaunt, sunken cheeks that photographed so well.

Behind her stood her husband, looking as if he wanted to turn and run the other way, but tethered by the bright red manicured talons she had dug into his arm.

"How *dare* you show your face at my benefit? You're responsible for the death of my baby."

Jason kept himself impassive in the face of her over-acting. If he hadn't seen her sans make-up, in tears, arms wrapped around herself as she rocked back and forth in her hospital room, he would have been hard pressed to take her melodrama seriously.

For the first time ever, he uttered one of the stock phrases he'd been forced to memorize during one of Sheffield Memorial's never-ending continuing education seminars. "I'm sorry for your loss."

He actually meant the sentiment. Another baby wasn't in this couple's future, no matter how much money they could throw at the problem.

"Sorry for my loss? Is that all you've got to say?"

Jason thought he'd done rather well.

She didn't give him time to search around for another platitude. "You killed my baby."

Stephanie pushed her way between him and the

woman. Good. He could use a bit of her diplomacy right now.

He waited for her magic words to make everything all right.

"Dr. Drake did *not* kill your baby." Her tone was fierce, almost snarling. Stephanie studied the woman from head to toe. "Poor prenatal care, undernourishment, and hiding the fact that you'd given birth before killed your baby. If we'd known early on we might have been able to use preventative measures to counteract the negative Rhesus factor. And sufficient maternal weight gain and bed-rest as your obstetrician recommended would have given your infant a better chance at survival. Even then your pregnancy would have been high risk. I explained all this when I first met with you and your team of lawyers, remember?"

Her husband looked confused. "Why didn't you tell *me* any of this?"

"You had to leave, remember? To get back on set before production costs went over-budget." The bitterness in her voice needed no theatrics to carry emotion.

Jason glared at the man. No husband should treat his wife so callously. The loss of a baby had psychological effects as well as physical effects. He'd read all the data that confirmed it.

The man shrugged off her explanation. "Is it true? Our baby wasn't your first?"

His wife's scrawny shoulders slumped. "I was young. It was a long time ago."

Jason knew he shouldn't get involved. "Cut her a break, man. Can't you see she's still grieving?"

All three of them looked at him as if he'd just grown another head.

The bartender pushed his way behind the curtain, catching Jason's attention.

He pointed to the microphone between them. "Dude. That thing's on."

CHAPTER FIVE

Panic overwhelmed Stephanie. She had just revealed her innermost, closely held angst to a room full of people who thought she had the perfect family—who thought she was the perfect daughter. And now they knew she resented every bite her nanny had ever fed to her from her silver spoon.

"Easy, there." Jason put his arm around her.

She should pull back, but she was none too stable on her feet.

"Get me out of here."

"Will do." He looked to the bartender. "Is there a back way out?"

The bartender pointed to a door behind them. "That leads to the parking lot."

In a mental fog, Stephanie was barely aware that Jason had picked her up and was carrying her out. The celebrity couple trailed behind them, making a quick getaway as well.

"I didn't realize Isaac's mother would be here. My attending probably wasn't such a great idea."

"I'd have to admit sensitivity isn't your middle name. Still, nothing like airing your dirty laundry over a loudspeaker."

Vaguely Stephanie worried about the host-essing dilemma their defection would cause the Montclairs and the Sheffields. She should be concerned about the heartache she had inadvertently caused her parents as well, but that damage was too deep to ponder.

When Jason held her tighter and murmured in her ear, "It will all eventually blow over," she realized she'd been whimpering.

As they looked out over an acre of luxury vehicles, Jason asked, "Where's your car?"

"Mother sent her car and driver for me." She was suddenly conscious of her weight in Jason's arms. "You can put me down now."

"You're not that heavy." He signaled for the attendant who had just arrived with the celebrities' limousine.

"Yes, sir?" The boy tried to look as if he saw women in red-spangled dresses being carried by tuxedoed men all the time. But the crack in his voice betrayed him.

"I need Dr. Montclair's driver."

The boy shuffled his feet. "I'm afraid he's not

here, sir. He left to run a quick errand and bring us all supper."

Jason turned so quickly Stephanie's already woozy head swam. "I guess that means you ride with me."

He started across the parking lot, his long, strong legs putting distance between her and her disgrace.

"Really, Jason, I can walk."

"We're almost there." He skirted a shiny black sports car, then stopped in front of his motorcycle. "Steady?"

"Yes. Put me down."

Slowly he lowered her feet, but held her tight against his chest. She should protest, but she didn't.

"Think you can hold on to me?"

Making her escape on the back of his low-slung motorcycle seemed absurdly funny. The giggle she couldn't hold back was tinged with hysteria. "I'm cold."

He whipped off his jacket and pushed her arms through the sleeves. "You're in shock."

He unstrapped his spare helmet and held it out to her.

"I can't. My hair." Stephanie tried to think of a solution but her brain was too muddled.

"Be still." He picked the pins from her hair, gently worked the band from her ponytail, then braided the long length faster than she could have done it herself.

"You're pretty good at that."

"Practice."

Jealousy broke through her fog. "You do this for women often?"

He grinned, smug and knowing. No sense in explaining that he'd braided three heads of hair every morning in one of the many foster homes he'd lived in. Instead of answering, he pushed the helmet onto her head.

"Chin up." With a finger, he lifted her chin, then fastened the strap.

Putting on his own helmet, he straddled the bike. Before he cranked it, he stopped. "Can you climb on by yourself?"

In answer, she hiked up her dress and swung her leg over the bike while he held it steady.

"Keep your legs away from the pipes." He pointed to the chrome exhaust pipes, well out of her way. "And hang on tight."

With that, he pulled out of the parking lot and onto the street.

Stephanie had never been on a motorcycle before. The power throbbed beneath her as Jason shifted gears, going faster and faster. The wind was both reviving and exhilarating. The nighttime lights blurred as they rushed by.

And, best of all, Jason felt warm and secure as she held him tight. If anyone were to ask, she would swear she could feel his own personal vibration revving through her.

All too soon he pulled into the parking garage at her apartment building. When he killed the motor her world became quiet—too quiet. And she could no longer block out the echo of her own words in her ears.

She had spouted all her childhood disappointments and fears to the entire ballroom, and she hadn't even gotten to the root of them. Up until her teens she'd had recurring nightmares that both her parents would rush to the hospital, leaving her alone for days on end in their big empty mansion with no one to care for her, having forgotten all about her while they were so deeply focused on their vocations.

As she'd got older she had rationalized away her fear, realizing that even if her bad dreams came true she could take care of herself.

But obviously her head had forgotten to tell her heart.

Now she had lashed out like the six-year-old she

had been when she hadn't had the words to define how desolate she felt.

And now everyone thought…

She would have to borrow a leaf from Jason's book and not worry about what everyone thought.

She didn't protest as he rode with her up in the elevator and then used his own key to open her door. By the time she stepped over the threshold she had her wits back.

She stopped him from entering. "It's been a long day."

"You're in shock," he said again.

"No. I'm fine now." She peeled off his coat, warm enough without it.

"Stephanie, we need to talk."

"I never thought to hear those words come out of *your* mouth, Jason Drake." She held up her hand to stop anything further he might add. "I only need two things from you. Get that physical and attend the sensitivity training class tomorrow, so I can add it to your personnel record."

Before he could protest she stepped back to close the door, but her world shifted under her as red spots floated in her vision.

Vertigo.

"Jason." She reached out. "Dizzy."

She felt his strong arms hold her, then let go, falling, falling into a bottomless black vortex.

As soon as Jason lay Stephanie on the floor she blinked back to consciousness.

Her skin felt clammy to his touch. Her face was pale, her eyes dilated. Her pulse had been thready, but now picked up the beat.

His own heartbeat settled back from his throat. He wished for water to wash the metallic taste of panic from his tongue but didn't dare leave her side.

He settled for licking his lips.

Brushing wispy strands from her loose braid back from her face, he said, "Hey," wanting to hear her voice in reply.

"Hey, back." She sounded fragile. Vulnerable. Very un-Stephanie-like. He wanted to gather her in his arms, but she didn't need jostling right now.

"What happened?" Her question carried strength, and a demand for answers. She struggled to sit as she attempted to focus past the confusion in her eyes.

He put his hand on her shoulder to keep her lying down, then took in a deep breath to break the tightness in his chest.

He'd done this to her. He'd let his passion get in

the way of his common sense and he'd gotten her pregnant. He'd taken the responsibility for birth control and he had failed. This was all his fault.

He didn't have to know his father to know the apple hadn't fallen far from the tree. Rotten to the core—like father, like son.

He clamped down on his own visceral reactions and focused on Stephanie.

"Be still." His hand on her bare shoulder looked so dark compared to her pallor. "You fainted."

Stephanie relaxed back. "You caught me before I fell?"

He nodded then affirmed with, "Yes."

Was she aware that her hand had covered his, trapping it firmly in place against her breast? Her other hand drifted to her belly, where their baby lay.

Jason watched the delicate lines of her throat as she swallowed, then said, "Thank you."

"How do you feel?"

Her focus went inward even as she met his eyes. "The dizziness is receding. No spots in my vision anymore. I don't feel as shaky as I did."

"Aside from the emotional turmoil, any other reasons for your fainting?"

"It's been a long day." Her stomach growled. "And I skipped lunch."

"Not a good idea."

"I had a consultation meeting with a demanding doctor."

She gave him a good-natured smirk by way of exoneration. Still, guilt burned through Jason's veins.

He pushed it out of the way. There was no place for emotions in emergencies.

He pulled his hand from hers and wrapped his fingers around her wrist to recheck her pulse. "Have you had problems with low blood sugar before?"

"How do you do that?" She lifted her arm to break the connection. "How do you make your eyes turn from the depths of the sky to the flatness of slate in only seconds?"

Her question struck like an arrowhead, finding a chink in his armor. He brushed away the pain.

"Speaking as your doctor, have you had any other incidents of syncope? Blood pressure problems? Shakiness?" His fingertips searched for the pulse in her throat. He found it gratifyingly steady and strong.

"Jason, you're not my doctor. I have a doctor."

He shouldn't upset a patient, but he had to ask. "Then who am I, Stephanie?"

Under his forefinger, her heart-rate picked up

speed and intensity while her eyes searched his. "Who do you want to be, Jason?"

Easy question. "I want to be your lover."

"Lover? You'll need to clarify for me." She held his gaze. "The man who makes love to me, or the man who loves me?"

Not so easy.

Make love? Yes. He wanted to make love to Stephanie—day and night.

When Stephanie stimulated his pleasure center his brain chemistry soaked up the dopamine which made his world better and brighter. That temporary high he got when his synapses and neurons popped always made him think clearer and faster and bigger—outside the box. Exactly the way a good diagnostician should do.

But love her? No, he could never love a woman—not even Stephanie. He'd tried that once in his foolish youth. Loving a woman made him reckless. Illogical. Ineffective. All traits that led to bad decisions. And a doctor who made bad decisions inadvertently killed people.

If his brother were still alive he would attest to that.

Despite his best effort, his eyes shifted from hers.

She blew out her breath. "Help me up. Lying flat like this, my back is starting to ache."

Grateful Stephanie had let him off the hook instead of demanding an answer, Jason helped her sit.

When she tried to stand, he stopped her. "Let me take off those shoes before you fall off them."

Holding her foot in his hand, he slipped off one spiked heel, then the other. His hands lingered on her ankles with enough of a caress that she would know he desired her. He was rewarded by the quickening of her breath, telling him the same.

"I'm going to miss these for the next several months." He rubbed his thumb along the arch of her foot and her eyes glazed with pleasure. As he had anticipated, she couldn't hold back her moan.

The way her body responded to him made his own blood rush through his veins.

She roused herself enough to protest. "I'll dress myself as I see best—like I've always done."

She pulled her feet from his grasp and started to stand.

He helped her up with more strength than grace. She ended up plastered to him, with her dress bunched up tight around her hips. His body couldn't help but respond as he breathed in the scent of her.

"Let me unzip you like I've wanted to do all night," he whispered in her ear.

She purred, and his desire for her hit him in the gut. Then her stomach growled again.

Food. He needed to get her blood sugar up before she fainted again. He had to think of her pregnancy.

A child—his child. In his head, he couldn't solidify the abstract concept into concrete reality.

"I think I need to stay the night to watch over you." He held her away from him. "It's the practical thing to do."

Stephanie blinked and saw the coldly sensible doctor in place of her blazing hot lover. Just like that, Jason could stuff all his passion back into its box. As if she didn't matter to him at all.

She stiffened and took a step away. Her head swam, but she refused to reach out to him and steady herself. How could she so easily confuse sex for something more? Jason would never wholly give himself to anyone, not even her—not in an emotional way.

"Just for tonight," she agreed.

It *was* the practical thing to do since she wasn't feeling that stable. Not that she could find her balance with Jason anymore. Her emotions for him kept her constantly off-center. She needed to get herself in check. To push her vulnerabilities to the side and be as in command as he was.

She turned her back to him. "Unzip me."

Yes, it was a taunt, but she needed to know. Needed to challenge herself and prove that her control over her physical attraction was as great as Jason's. Needed to prove that she could turn on and off her yearning for him as he could his for her.

He worked the zipper down, his warm fingers barely touching her skin, and she knew she'd lost the challenge.

Then she turned. With a great deal of satisfaction she saw it in his eyes. Desire. So he had lost the challenge, too.

Good to know that he ached for her as much as she ached for him.

"I'm hungry." She let all the implications of her hunger come through the huskiness in her voice. "You promised to feed me." For added effect she ran her tongue along her lip.

Jason's Adam's apple bobbled twice before he growled out, "Go change clothes while I make supper."

She looked down, saw his hands spasmodically clench and unclench, and smiled, making sure he knew that she knew.

"Stephanie..." It was a warning with an edge.

She pushed her own limits as she trailed her hand

along the pearl buttons on his shirt. "Something spicy, please."

Then she turned on her heel and walked away, feeling his eyes bore through her, but she resisted turning back.

Score one for Stephanie.

CHAPTER SIX

As soon as she was out of Jason's sight exhaustion overpowered her. He felt only sexual attraction—a very powerful sexual attraction—but it was only skin-deep between them.

A woman needed more than good sex to sustain a relationship. She needed to know she was cherished as well as desired. And a child needed total, absolute, unconditional love to thrive.

Claiming responsibility for a child wasn't enough, but that was all Jason had to offer. Or at least all he was willing to offer.

Stephanie dredged up the will to wash off her make-up and replace contacts with glasses. Without thought she reached for her favorite T-shirt and gym shorts. She didn't bother to hang up her dress. She planned to burn it in the morning.

Jason made kitchen noises followed by delicious aromas. As empty as her pantry was, she wondered what he had found to cook. But he was a whiz at that sort of thing.

"About done in there?" Jason called from the kitchen.

Her pride urged her to tell him to leave. But her heart begged to let him stay.

Maybe she could find resignation to the fact that there could be no deep relationship between them?

"I'm on my way."

Jason had set her tiny kitchen table with a linen tablecloth and matching napkins, and full place-settings of china, silverware, and crystal goblets inherited from her great-grandmother. As a centerpiece a pristine white taper from her den's fireplace mantel flickered in a silver candleholder, next to her ceramic everyday salt and pepper shakers, incongruous among the unaccustomed finery.

That was how she felt in her worn oversized sleep shirt and gym shorts. Incongruous. But a negligee would have been playing with a fire she didn't have the energy to contain.

What did it matter in the end? There could be nothing between them. Her life would be made simpler by making a clean cut from Jason and raising her baby alone.

She ignored the wave of sadness that rode in on that lonesome thought and straightened her spine with Montclair independence.

Very properly, she said, "Everything looks nice. And it smells delicious. Thank you, Jason."

He smiled with a hint of strain at the corners of his mouth. "I thought we'd celebrate our happy occasion."

"*Are* you, Jason? Are you happy?" She took a long look into those guarded eyes, at those too-stiff shoulders, that rigid stillness. He looked like a man standing on the rim of a volcano, ready to fling himself over the edge as a sacrifice for the greater good.

"I take care of my own. It's my responsibility and my right." He said it as if he dared her to dispute it.

Not tonight. She'd fought too many battles for one day. She broke their stare first, looking down at the meal he had prepared for her.

On her plate sat a fluffy yellow omelet, filled with tiny white and orange-hued shrimp and seasoned with flecks of green herbs. On a side plate rested toast spread with cream cheese and orange marmalade—her favorite. The crystal flutes were filled with a clear liquid that fizzed.

"Ginger ale," Jason answered before she could ask. "Breakfast for supper. It's all I could find."

"It's perfect."

He lifted a glass.

It would have been churlish not to follow suit.

"To our child," he said.

If she hadn't known him so intimately she wouldn't have noticed that small hesitation in his voice before he said the word *child*. Her throat thickened, but she saluted with her glass and swallowed nevertheless.

They ate in silence. Only two weeks ago the room would have felt light and tranquil without unnecessary small talk between them. Tonight it was heavy with the weightiness of unspoken and unacknowledged feelings.

If the meal hadn't been so delicious Stephanie wouldn't have been able to eat a single bite. For the sake of her baby—and her baby's father—she tried.

As Jason finished his last bit of toast she counted to ten out of politeness—before bolting from the table.

"You cooked. I'll clean," she said. They had fallen into that arrangement the first time they'd shared a meal—the night they'd first made love.

"I'll take care of it." He rose, plates in hand.

She tried to lighten the mood. "That's not very fair, is it?"

"What's not fair is giving you an unplanned baby."

She looked away from the regret in his eyes.

She had no regrets. "I'm pregnant, not an invalid."

"You lost consciousness."

He knelt at her feet and looked into her eyes. She looked for warmth. All she saw was determination.

"I'll take care of you, Stephanie. You and the baby."

Out of obligation. But obligation wouldn't provide the loving environment she was determined to create for her child.

His cell phone on the counter vibrated. For a split second he glanced toward it, the desire to answer that call clearly in his eyes, before he turned back to her. But the intensity of his focus was now diluted as his thoughts drifted to the beep that signaled a voicemail message.

"Jason, there's no need. I'm fully capable of taking care of both myself and my baby. Now, go answer your phone."

"I won't be but a second." He was standing and turning away before he'd even completed his sentence.

While he took the call Stephanie washed and dried the dishes, folded the tablecloth and napkins for the laundry and blew out the candle.

By the time he was finished she was sitting on

her couch, pretending to read a magazine and wishing he would just go.

Urgent call finished, Jason laid his cell phone on the coffee table and joined Stephanie on the couch.

She really should tell him to walk away now, before he could tell her that duty called and he had to leave. It was a dignity thing.

Then he slid his arm around her shoulders, pulling her tight into his side. The heat of his body warmed the cold place deep inside her chest.

"So you're staying?"

"I said I would. I won't leave you by yourself tonight." He frowned. "That was Dr. Phillips calling for you. When she couldn't reach you, she called me."

"Couldn't reach me?" That was when Stephanie remembered her red-sequined clutch with her cell phone in it lay on the back seat of her mother's car. "So she assumed you would be here with me? How fast has word spread?"

"At Sheffield? Faster than a virus in a daycare center. But Phillips didn't say anything personal. Just that she'd been calling you and finally reached a point where her request was critical, so she called me." He hugged her to him. "Not to worry. It was just an administrative problem. Dr. Phillips wanted authority to order an MRI on her patient before she recommended surgery. As Senior Fellow for the department, I gave her permission and took care of the problem for you."

If she didn't know better, she would believe that his arm around her could protect her from the world.

But she was made of sterner stuff. "I can take care of my own problems. I'm a Montclair, Jason. I stand firmly on my own two feet."

"I seem to remember a recent fainting episode…." He raised an eyebrow.

She couldn't stop the corner of her mouth from twitching. "Figuratively, if not always literally. And that was an aberration."

No one but Jason had ever teased her before. From the beginning he'd seen beneath her reserved exterior to the hidden part of her that longed to share a laugh with her colleagues but didn't know how.

One of the things that had most attracted her to him was the fact that Jason brought out her lighter side and let her feel comfortable with it.

Stephanie snuggled more securely into him before she realized what she had done, so she made her tone harsh, showing him she meant business. "I was right here, Jason. You could have handed the phone to me."

He responded by tickling her neck with the ends of her own hair. "Then you don't mind everyone at the hospital knowing we're back together?"

"We're not back together." Trapped firmly in his embrace, with no will to move away, she knew her declaration didn't ring as true as it might have.

Jason did the moving away. But only far enough to look her in the eyes. "Stephanie, you're carrying my child. That binds us together—forever. We really need to stop denying what's between us and be adults about our relationship."

"Relationship. New word in your vocabulary?"

He smiled. "Yes. It is."

But his smile didn't reach his eyes. Instead, worry creased his forehead. He cocooned her hand in both of his. "Stephanie, how do you feel about this baby?"

As if she'd been waiting for him to ask, answers she hadn't even put into words bubbled up. "At first I panicked. The idea of having a baby totally overwhelmed me."

How did she explain?

"My time with you was supposed to be a summer fling—an experience I've never indulged in before." She felt her cheeks heat up at that confession. But she wanted complete honesty between them. "You were a reward for my finally achieving a place in my profession where…"

"Where what, Stephanie?"

Where she felt worthy of her parents' pride. But honesty didn't stretch to revealing *all* her insecurities. "Before you, I had been so career-focused. I decided it was time to have a little fun." Aside from the mandatory escort to various social events, she'd never really dated that much—another thing he didn't need to know.

"So I was just supposed to be your boy toy?"

"No!" *Honesty, Stephanie.* She ducked her head. "Yes."

Jason twirled a lock of her hair around his finger and grinned. "I can live with that." Then he looked down, clenching and unclenching his free fist. "No, I can't. That night at the cabin, I should have—"

"No, Jason. We both should have. Shared act, shared accountability." Stephanie covered his tense hand. "I've thought about this. I'm a reasonably intelligent woman, wouldn't you say?"

He gave her a quirky smile. "More than reasonably."

"I know all the ways to prevent pregnancy, including the morning-after pill, but I chose not to go that route. Maybe not consciously, but certainly subconsciously."

"What are you saying, Stephanie?"

"A baby hadn't been in my plans. But now I have new plans. Better plans. Plans for a future full of nurturing and love." Instinctively she covered her belly with her hand. Now, with the world knowing about her pregnancy, she wouldn't have to remember to hide her intuitive gesture. "I can't imagine my life without my child in it."

"*Our* child, Stephanie. Our child." The set of his jaw brooked no argument. "This is shared parenthood. My responsibility as much as yours. I know you don't need my money, but I fully intend to contribute to our child's upbringing."

"A child needs more than money. The best nanny money can buy isn't enough. A child needs a parent she can count on to always be there."

"How are you going to manage that? Give up your career to hover over a crib twenty-four-seven? What about the times you're on call?"

Stephanie had been mulling over that issue ever since she'd seen the positive sign on the pregnancy test stick. There had to be a way. "Things have to change. My child will always be first in my life. I'm not going to run out the door every time the phone rings."

"Are you saying I will?"

"Your past record strongly indicates yes, Jason." She felt a deep-seated anger growing inside her. "How many times have I finished dinner alone while you caught a cab from the restaurant? How many movies have you seen through to the end with me? I didn't even suggest attending a play or a concert because of the disruption you'd make threading through the theater seats during the performance. Even when we have good, reliable staff on call, any time your cell phone rings you're gone."

She searched for Jason's reaction, looking for an indication that he understood. All she saw was his stony lack of emotion. As an adult, she knew he was only guarding his own vulnerability. But would a child understand? Or would their baby think he truly didn't care? It was a look she never wanted her child to have to live with.

"You were wrong about the phone call earlier," he said, and his eyes reflected a cold challenge. "That one was for you. What would you have done if it had been your patient in a life-or-death situation?"

She still had five and a half months to figure it out, but so far she had no solution.

Before she could come up with a suitable retort, Jason wrapped his fingers around her wrist.

"Jason—"

"Shh!" He counted her pulse. "Your blood pressure's up. We'll change the subject."

"Or you could leave."

"Not tonight." He stood and moved away to the recliner, grabbed the television remote from the side table and surfed channels until he found a documentary on white-water rapids.

As if they had never exchanged heated words between them, he asked, "This okay with you?"

How could he do that? How could he box up his emotions so tightly and put them behind him? Or maybe she was wrong. Maybe he truly felt nothing after all—except for sexual desire.

She could make him go. If she insisted, he would respect her wishes. If she weren't so tired she would evict him. Wouldn't she?

But, truth be told, her syncope really worried her. Blood pressure problems seemed to be plaguing her pregnancy.

As Stephanie glanced at Jason, firmly ensconced in her armchair, his attention focused on the television, she couldn't deny the false sense of security having him around gave her.

She picked up the magazine she'd laid down earlier, determined to demonstrate how much she didn't need him.

The words in the article swam together as eyestrain took its toll. She would close her eyes for a second, let them rest and refocus. Her eyelids drifted downward. The darkness was soothing, relaxing. She didn't even try to hold back her yawn.

Her next thought was that Jason must have stayed the night.

His sleepy, musky scent wafted from the pillow she hugged so tightly.

Vaguely she remembered stirring when he carried her to bed, and again when he held her close to take away her shivers.

The sun beamed in at her window—proof she'd slept until almost noon. She hadn't slept so long or so well, hadn't felt so rested, since—since the three-week cruise her parents had given her as a medical school graduation present. Even then she'd felt the constant edge of being a single in a couples' environment.

For a while Jason had made that lonely sensation go away.

But this morning he was gone and it was back.

She picked up her glasses on the bedside table to read his note.

Breakfast in the fridge.

How did she reconcile his acts of kindness and thoughtfulness with his display of unyielding stoicism?

Her stomach gave a happy rumble at the sight of fresh strawberries and blackberries in a bowl, next to a cup of yogurt topped with granola—evidence that he'd taken an early-morning walk to the organic food store down the block. Wearing last night's tuxedo, how many eyebrows had he raised?

Not as many as she had raised last night, she'd bet.

She forced herself to eat, hoping the yogurt would help to settle a stomach that revolted at last night's memories. She would need all her strength and sustenance to face the next few days and the consequences of her public confession of the heart.

CHAPTER SEVEN

JASON sat by himself in the back row of the sensitivity training class, earnestly trying to pay attention. But his mind kept wandering.

He prided himself on being flexible, taking whatever life threw at him, but this fatherhood thing had him taken aback.

A baby. Not just any baby but *his* baby.

He had never expected to be a father. He certainly would never have chosen fatherhood, not wanting to subject a child to his lack of family skills. Could character flaws be inherited? He'd never read any definitive research, but then it had never been that important to him until now.

But now, as unworthy as he might be, he would do everything in his power to be the best father he could. He sincerely hoped his best would be good enough.

With renewed determination, he focused on the instructor.

"Class, let's do an exercise to put us more in

touch with our feelings." The counselor clicked a new image onto the lecture room screen. "In your notebook you'll see a list of emotions. Quickly, without giving the words much thought, circle the ones that apply to you at this moment."

The list read: "Happy. Angry. Surprised. Fearful. Needy. Hopeful. Anxious. Bored."

Within seconds, Jason had the assignment completed.

He studied the results. He'd drawn thick, bold lines around all but 'Angry' and 'Bored'.

Before last night, those would have been the only two emotions circled.

Amazing how a baby, months away from delivery, had changed his life overnight.

"Everyone think about what you've circled. Is this where you want to be in your life?" The instructor looked smug, as if he had it all figured out. What would this overconfident trained counselor do with Jason's news?

"Now, class, write down three concrete goals—simple sentences will do—on what you'd like to change about your life."

Change? Jason had enough change to deal with without inventing anymore.

How did Stephanie feel about the baby—*their* baby?

He thought through last night's scenario, as he'd done a hundred times since dropping her off at her apartment. Too many things had happened too quickly to sort out her reactions to any of them.

This morning he'd reached for the phone a dozen times, driven past her apartment on his way to the hospital, strolled past her dark, empty office right before class, but he hadn't followed through on making contact.

What did he say? *You've made me the most off-balance, confused, ecstatic, scared stiff—circle all the emotions that apply—that I've been in my whole life?*

Jason bet that even their highly qualified instructor wouldn't have the words for this life-changing occasion.

Life. He and Stephanie had created life—right there inside her womb. The concept overwhelmed him.

"Everyone done?"

No. I'm just getting started, Jason thought. He'd have a child to raise, to nurture, to guide.

Damn. He had no idea how to do any of that. He'd better stop by the bookstore on the way home and pick up some research material.

The instructor called to the class. "Now, let's

role-play. Turn to the person next to you and get acquainted."

Jason turned to find Mike seated next to him. When had he slid into class? And why?

Mike should have some of the answers Jason needed.

"What are you doing here?"

They both ignored the instructor, who told them to read from the script in their handouts, finish the incomplete sentences, then take a break.

Mike gave him an awkward smile. "I was just walking by."

Jason didn't believe him for a second. "Yeah, right. Tell me another one."

Mike grinned, ignoring Jason's sarcasm. "Rough night?"

"I've had better." Jason looked down at his list of circled words. "So the rumors are already circulating?"

"I got a text last night from a friend of a friend. Is it true?"

"Is what true?"

"Dr. Stephanie Montclair is pregnant with your baby?"

"Yes, it's true." A sense of pride overcame him, despite knowing their slip-up had put Stephanie in a very awkward position.

Mike slapped him on the shoulder. "Congratulations, Dad. You're going to love parenthood."

An infusion of joy raced through Jason's veins, giving him an ecstatic dizziness as if he'd just scaled a mountain and his head was now in the clouds.

He brought himself back down to earth by thinking of how Stephanie wanted to shut him out of her life and her baby's life—*his* baby's life.

"She doesn't want me—" he had to swallow hard to get out the rest "—involved as the baby's father. She's pretty certain I'll do more harm than good."

"Then you'll have to convince her otherwise."

"What if she's right?"

Mike scanned the room, as if looking for the right words to say. He finally focused back on Jason. "My kids love you. Every kid who comes through your department loves you. They all sense your strength, your constancy, your care for their wellbeing. All those qualities will be intensified the first time you hold your child. Or the kid calls you Daddy. Or you have to clean his first skinned knee."

"Aren't you afraid of screwing it up?"

"Hell, yeah. But my wife tells me that's what

makes me a good father. I keep trying to get it right." Mike grinned. "And some days I think I do."

"My track record's not that great."

"You've got other kids?"

"Let's just say I've been in the parental role before. It didn't work out too well."

"I've known you a long time, Jason. Was this during those teenaged years you won't talk about?"

When Jason said nothing in response, Mike jostled him. "All kids deserve a father. This kid deserves *you* for a father. Don't let your child down before it's even born."

The pain of abandonment that Jason had tried to deny all his life crashed in on him.

If his own parents hadn't wanted him, how did he convince Stephanie to want him?

But for the sake of his child he had to try.

The instructor came back in, ready to continue his mind-probing exercises.

Mike leaned over and whispered. "Hey, friend, I've got to go. Need to buy a doll and a pretty gift sack to stick it in before the birthday party. But call me if you want to talk."

"Yeah, sure." What was all this talking stuff? As if *that* would fix anything. Still… "Thanks."

"I'm here for you, Jason."

When had that happened? When had Mike become such a good friend? And how could Jason have missed it?

More proof that he was no good at this relationship stuff.

He turned his attention back to the screen, but held little hope that a two-hour class would teach him how to be good enough for Stephanie and her family.

Once he'd completed the class, he snagged a resident and insisted on a quick physical. This time his blood pressure and heart-rate stayed in the proper range. Stephanie should be pleased—at least that he'd followed orders if not that he was in good health.

After a couple of quick shopping stops he drove home, prepared to spend the rest of the weekend doing hard labor to work out the pent-up energy that made his mind race in endless circles.

Sunday night he dropped into bed, hoping he was finally exhausted enough to sleep. Despite the hours he'd spent pounding on his roof, replacing shingles and tightening gutters, he was no closer to clearing his head.

He lay in the dark, remembering that Stephanie was giving him an easy way out.

The clock blinked as the minutes passed. He put his pillow over his head to block the annoying light but he couldn't block the decisions that plagued him.

Hell. When had he ever done things the easy way?

Stephanie's parents had been more than gracious in accepting her apology. With their bigger-than-life personalities, neither had realized their quiet, studious daughter had felt unimportant and overlooked.

Hearing how much her parents loved her, even when they had never really understood her, had begun to heal a lot of wounds.

After the emotional weekend with her parents, and an emergency meeting with the hospital's lawyers to plan damage control in case the celebrity couple sued for her breach of confidentiality, Stephanie braced herself for the most difficult Monday she'd ever had.

For the hundredth time she wondered what Jason had done with the rest of his weekend. Every time her cell phone had rung her heart had raced at the thought that he might be calling.

But he never had.

For which she was grateful. She had enough problems to juggle. Right?

Running late due to the morning sickness that

had reappeared this morning, Stephanie pulled into her assigned slot in the staff parking garage next to Jason's motorcycle.

Dressed in a conservative navy sheath and matching sweater, with classic pearls, she climbed from her car. Her exit wasn't as graceful as she would wish for. The low-slung vehicle would play hell with her dignity as her size increased.

And what was it about telling the world she was pregnant that made her waist grow three inches overnight? The sheath and two other loose-waisted dresses were all that would fit this morning.

As she grabbed her purse, the reality she had been ignoring threatened to overwhelm her. Everyone at the hospital now knew. Those who had only guessed were now positive. She'd had a fling with Jason Drake and now she carried his baby.

They would whisper behind her back. Judge her lack of control, her inability to handle her personal affairs. Wonder if she was competent enough to do her job or if it had been nepotism all along.

Nonsense. She'd earned her sterling reputation through years of hard work. Her personal life had nothing to do with her professionalism at the hospital. If anyone doubted that, she would soon prove them wrong by her actions.

Stephanie raised her chin, pasted on her social smile and went to work, blaming her lapse in confidence on the hormones coursing through her body. Advice from her mother: blame everything on the hormones.

Marcy greeted her with poorly hidden curiosity in her eyes, which Stephanie firmly ignored.

On her desk she found the Certificate of Completion for Jason's sensitivity class, a copy of the findings in his recent physical and a shoebox with a card attached.

"For the baby" was scrawled in Jason's outrageous handwriting.

Inside was a lovely pair of ballet-style flats, bright red and butter-soft, with good insole support. They were the right size.

She should give them back. Shoes were too personal for the strictly professional relationship she intended to establish.

For the baby. Was that a challenge? A statement of his parental rights? Or just a thoughtful gift that emphasized his medical advice to stay off the stilettos.

She would give them back and buy her own shoes.

But trying them on wouldn't hurt, would it?

Perfect fit. As she walked around her office the slight nagging twinge in her back went away.

She wiggled her toes.

The thought of squeezing her restrictive dress pumps back onto her slightly swollen feet made her wince. She would wear the red flats around her office this morning, until she had time to run out at lunchtime and buy her own pair. Then back they would go—along with her own note saying "thanks, but no thanks."

Opening her files, she set to work reassigning her patients among Drs. Riser and Phillips. Recruiting a new pulmonary specialist and supervising Jason's workload would be enough.

The solution to the lawsuit that had seemed so perfect at the time seemed so wrong now. She'd thought Jason would just shrug it off. Instead she'd wounded him deeply.

Marcy buzzed the intercom. "Dr. Montclair? You're needed in Maggie Malone's room as soon as possible."

She heard the child's screams as she rounded the corner. Not taking time to knock, she pushed open Maggie's door to the commotion inside.

Stephanie had to squeeze her way into the room past an attending nurse, a new resident she'd recently assigned to Dr. Riser, and Dr. Riser himself to get to Jason.

Like a major general, Jason stood in the middle of the chaos, giving orders to everyone in attendance.

"We need to get her body temperature down. *Now.* Get those layers of clothing off her and wrap her in the thermal blanket," he said, moments before the monitor dinged an alarm.

He spoke with such authority and urgency the nurse and the resident collided rushing for the blanket.

Jason pointed to the nurse. "Don't you understand the word *now*?"

The nurse looked dazed and confused.

Jason lifted Maggie from her mother's lap, pulled off her heavy flannel nightgown, socks and knit cap, took the chilled blanket Stephanie held ready for him and wrapped Maggie without waiting for anyone else's compliance.

Maggie screamed, not happy with her treatment or the pandemonium around her.

"What are you doing?" Dr. Riser grabbed for Maggie.

Like an iceberg in turbulent seas, Jason stood stalwart. "I'm cooling her off." His deep voice undercut the girl's shrieks.

The monitor showed her temperature had spiked to 105 degrees Fahrenheit.

Dr. Riser pointed down to the discarded clothes on the floor. "You're the one who warmed her up."

The blanket was working. The girl's body temperature had already dropped a half-degree.

"Because her mother said she couldn't remember the last time her daughter sweat." He glared at Anne who was wringing her hands together in the corner, obviously distressed.

Stephanie grimaced. Drake's statement sounded like an accusation of neglect to her. Anne had been at her daughter's bedside night and day for over a week, and according to the girl's charts took excellent care of her daughter.

Information about the child's perspiration tendencies might be crucial, but couldn't Jason have used the slightest bit of tact when soliciting it?

She would address that later. Now she had a crisis to manage.

Stephanie put her hand on Dr. Riser's outstretched arm. Deliberately putting quiet steel in her voice, she said, "Stand down, Dr. Riser. This is Dr. Drake's case."

Dr. Riser gave her a curt nod before crossing his arms and moving aside to glare at Jason.

As soon as the monitor registered another half-degree cooler Jason unwrapped Maggie's arms and handed her the doll she'd been holding earlier. She immediately put the doll's hand in her mouth, quieting her cries.

He swept the circle of attendants with a glance, then pointed to the resident. "You—go and get the popsicle I promised her. Make it fast. Then meet me back in the consulting room."

He handed Maggie to her mother and left the room without a backward glance, confident Stephanie and Dr. Riser would follow him out.

Instead, Stephanie stayed behind to smooth ruffled feathers. Her department didn't need another lawsuit right now—especially since she was trying to untangle the one they already had.

"My apologies for Dr. Drake. He comes across rough, but he's one of the best," she said to Anne.

"Dr. Montclair, if this hospital spent less time trying to censor Dr. Drake's bedside manner and more time recognizing his drive and determination we'd all be better off."

Stephanie was taken aback at this mild woman's defense of Jason. It had rarely—make that never— happened before.

Anne put her daughter into the bed, then turned, hands on hips, and squared off. "Dr. Drake is the only professional I've met who hasn't patted us on the head, given us platitudes, then passed us on to someone else because his ego couldn't handle not being able to figure out what was wrong. Why doesn't Dr. Drake's own hospital value him as much as we do?"

"Sheffield Memorial *does* value Dr. Drake."

"Not from what I'm seeing. I heard one of the nurses say everything he does has to be approved by you. And then Dr. Riser comes in and questions his methods in front of that young resident. You've got a problem with your staff, Dr. Montclair, but it's not Dr. Drake. I wouldn't blame him for leaving Sheffield Memorial." She paused, visibly trying to get her emotions under control.

"Dr. Drake isn't leaving." Stephanie's heart skipped a beat. But wasn't that what she wanted? Jason gone so she could raise her child alone?

What would her life be like without Jason Drake in it, for her as well as for her child?

Empty. The word echoed from her heart. Nonsense. *Empty of complications* was what she'd meant to think. *Stable and uncomplicated* also came immediately to mind.

She'd had a life before Jason Drake. She would have an even fuller one after him—thanks to the child she carried.

Jason's child.

She brushed away the wayward thought. Her subconscious was not her friend today. Or maybe it was her hormones making her overly sensitive. But that was her personal life.

She needed to pull herself together. She hadn't worked this hard to become Department Director to let her personal life get in the way now.

"Why would he stay?" Anne gave her a hard stare. "If I were Dr. Drake I would be looking for someone who believed in me, who trusted me, who respected me. But then again, it looks to me like you're trying to push him away before he can leave. Is it because of the baby?"

"The baby?" Instinctively Stephanie put her hand over her stomach. "Of course not."

But she had been. She had been pushing him away ever since that night under the stars—the night the baby had been conceived, the night she'd realized she was falling for him.

Why was she pushing him away?

So he won't leave me first. So I can deal with the loss on my own terms. It made no sense, but then matters of the heart rarely did.

"I've read all about that celebrity baby. Everything I've seen says it's not Dr. Drake's fault."

Oh. That baby. Stephanie slid her hand into the

pocket of her lab coat. "Dr. Drake put his heart and soul into trying to save that little life. Without getting into confidentiality issues, all I can say is that sometimes things just happen."

Anne nodded in agreement. "Anyone can see the fire in Dr. Drake's eyes when he's trying to make a child better. He could give up breathing easier than he could give up medicine. How could you chastise a man of such passion and caring?"

Anne had confused caring with obsession. Jason hated to lose a case. It was personal pride. Just as he took personal pride in lovemaking—an obsession Stephanie had certainly benefited from.

"I assure you, Anne, Dr. Drake's passion is one of his most valued traits." An image of Jason naked in her arms, face flushed with passion, invaded Stephanie's mind. "Sheffield holds Dr. Drake in the highest regard."

Anne seemed a bit mollified. "Once Dr. Drake commits, he doesn't abandon. Not ever. He gives his whole heart."

Stephanie thought of the many times Jason had been called heartless by the staff. Yes, doctors had to be stoic to be effective, but Jason carried it to an extreme, claiming emotion had no place in diagnosis.

Anne obviously saw what she wanted to see. It

wasn't unusual for a family member to develop a case of hero-worship for their child's healthcare professional. A temporary attachment was generally harmless as long as the healthcare professional stayed remote and professional—a talent Jason excelled at.

Why, then, did Stephanie feel a jealous possessiveness she had no reason to feel? *Because she didn't want anyone else to defend him. That was her job.*

Stephanie took a step toward the door. "Thank you for your endorsement of Dr. Drake. I'll be sure to pass on your compliments."

Anne collapsed into the bedside chair, all the fervor gone from her eyes. "I'm sorry. My psychologist would say I was projecting. This is the anniversary of my divorce and I'm taking out my hurt and anger on you. Raising a child by myself is just so hard sometimes. But then, we're not talking personal relationships, are we? Dr. Drake is probably taking this lawsuit thing in stride. I'm sure professional relationships are handled differently."

"Not so much," Stephanie admitted through stiff lips as a shiver ran down her spine. "If you'll excuse me, I've got duties."

She walked out of Maggie's room with her mind whirling.

Pushing open the consulting room door, she found Jason inside, pouring himself a cup of coffee while waiting for her.

"Dr. Riser and his sidekick have come and gone. They had nothing to add to Maggie's case," he told her. He held up an empty mug. "Tea?"

"Yes, thanks."

Jason put the water on to boil as he stirred cream into his coffee. Digging through the teabags, he pulled out a herbal concoction. "Caffeine-free."

He said it as a statement more than a question, so she didn't bother to answer.

So many issues. Where did she begin?

She thought about taking her usual seat at the conference table. No, dealing with Jason Drake was best done on her feet.

Maybe he wouldn't notice the red shoes she hadn't taken time to change when she'd been summoned to Maggie's room. She should have never put them on. He would read more into her acceptance of the gift than she meant him to.

Of course Jason caught her glance downward to her feet.

She would start there.

"Jason, thank you for the gift, but let's keep our personal lives away from the hospital. I don't intend to broadcast my pregnancy."

"Like you did last Friday night? You're a few days too late for that, little momma." He stared at her baby bump as if he had X-ray vision. "I'll not deny my child, Stephanie."

"I'll not have my authority undermined because people think our past relationship gives you an advantage over them."

His sharp laugh scraped as painful as barbed wire. "Advantage, Stephanie? What advantage would that be? From Dr. Riser's behavior, it's clear to everyone I'm *persona non grata* around here."

"He shouldn't have questioned you in front of a patient. I'll talk to him." Stephanie would need to do something about Dr. Riser. He was a good doctor, but Jason was the Senior Fellow of Diagnostics and he would stay that way. Dr. Riser's assertive attitude was starting to cross the line from healthy competition to undermining jealousy. Not an unusual powerplay in a hospital setting, and one she'd handled easily enough before. But she'd never been involved with one of the players before.

Was Jason even capable of feeling something deeper for her? Or was she only judging him by the emotionless façade he showed everyone else? Why had she never taken a good long look past his protective shell?

The answer was too obvious to ignore. Because

she'd wanted to isolate herself from any potential hurt their relationship might cause her.

"I take care of my own problems." A muscle in Jason's jaw throbbed as if he were forcing the conversation through clenched teeth.

"Jason, you're Senior Fellow, but I'm Department Director. I'll take care of Dr. Riser."

"Like you took care of the lawsuit? No, thanks." He looked as dispassionate as if he were discussing milk or sugar for her tea. But his clenched fist around his coffee cup told a different story.

"I thought…." She dropped into her chair. What had she thought?

Deep down, she'd thought Jason was too arrogant to care what anyone thought of him. Even her.

On some level had she done it to punish him for all those missed dates? For the heartache he'd caused by making her second on his priority scale?

"Stephanie, was it you who gave the hospital labs instructions this morning to hold all my orders for running diagnostic tests? Has the pharmacy been told the same. Have all my privileges been revoked?"

"Not revoked. Just under my signature." She licked her lips, wishing she had the cup of tea to hide behind.

"Not much difference there." As if he read her

mind, Jason slid the cup in front of her. Hot tea sloshed over the side, pooling on the clean surface of the consult table. Although his face didn't show it, Jason's lack of precise control stood testament to the magnitude of his anger.

"Sign me off for unrestricted privileges."

"Jason, you know we can't do it that way." She drew an X through the cooling liquid as her conscience pricked once again. Agreeing to that settlement had been a way to gain personal approval from the board—a board that consisted primarily of family and friends.

"We all know the lawsuit is a farce."

"I've signed my name to the agreement. I can't treat it lightly. If I purposely ignore the agreement our whole department could be sanctioned."

He walked to the window, his back to her. "You've taken away the tools of my trade."

She didn't need to hear the flatness of his voice to understand how deeply she had hurt him.

"I made a mistake. I'm sorry. I'll talk to the lawyers and do everything I can to correct it." On the verge of tears, her voice broke. Damned hormones.

She hesitated to add more, but did anyway. "Jason, I might have taken away your hospital privileges, but I could never take away your mind."

"If only that were true." He said it so quietly she almost thought she'd imagined it.

As if nothing had happened between them, he walked over to his whiteboard, picked up the marker and circled *'inability to perspire'* on the list that had been marked up and crossed through a dozen times over the last few days. "We can rule out all forms of muscular dystrophy. Too many symptoms don't fit. I think we need to look into chromosomal DNA testing."

She needed time to process, to think. For now, she wrapped herself in the tatters of professionalism and pretended it was business as usual. "Those tests are expensive. I'll have Marcy check their insurance coverage."

"So now Marcy has to approve my decisions, too?" He pointed to a ragged overflowing folder on the table between them. "Maggie and her mother have a private fund that will make sure the tests are covered. It's in Maggie's file."

"I only meant…." What had she meant? That she needed that last fragment of control?

Stephanie was starting to take a long hard look at herself, and she wasn't liking what she saw at all. "Let me know which tests and I'll make sure the order goes through." The alarm on her cell phone buzzed but she ignored it.

Jason didn't. He glanced at his watch. "Lunchtime."

"I ate a big breakfast, if you want to keep working."

"You need to eat regularly, Stephanie. No more skipping meals. You've got our child to feed."

Our child. Proof that she and Jason would always be tied together. It was time to stop pushing him away and start repairing the damage she had done. "Want to join me?"

Jason stood and walked to the door. "I've got plans."

"Plans?"

"Personal plans. I won't be back today." As he pulled the door closed behind him the click of the latch sounded loud in the silent conference room.

CHAPTER EIGHT

FOR the first time in memory Jason pulled his motorcycle into his parking slot to see Stephanie's red sports car already in her assigned space.

Making that spur-of-the-moment decision to run in the charity half-marathon yesterday had been a spontaneous choice that was unlike him, but it had produced excellent results. After thirteen miles of pounding the pavement he'd been tired enough to sleep the night through, even past his alarm. No tossing and turning, thinking of a particular woman who thought enough of him to sleep with him but not enough to share parenting with him.

Stuck to the center of his computer monitor was a note in Stephanie's handwriting. He was being summoned—in a polite Montclair way. At his convenience, she'd said.

Nothing about her was convenient.

But then he'd always found convenient to be boring.

He would take Stephanie's request at face value

and work her into his schedule. Unapologetically, Maggie came first today.

After forty-five minutes of playing phone tag with doctors across the world, Jason found the chromosomal DNA expert he was looking for in New York, at Mount Sinai Medical Center.

The doctor was in a meeting, so he left a message, feeling one step closer to finding the answer to Maggie's condition.

The hurry-up-and-wait game of diagnostics always tested his patience, but the win in the end made it worth it.

Except when he lost.

Like with Stephanie.

He wasn't sure what he'd wanted to win. But now it didn't matter. Now he understood there was no future for them—only shared custody of their child and medicine. And he'd fight her for his right to practice both of those privileges until his dying breath.

As he sat in her office, waiting for her to emerge from her *en suite* restroom, he braced himself to keep from letting his gut response to Stephanie overrule his logic.

Remembering the flattering offer from the Mayo soothed his ego. Men made long-distance fatherhood work all the time. He'd have to check into how they did it. He would never abandon his child, or his child's mother, no matter how angry she made him, but maybe he could find a way to have it all.

Yes, he was furious with Stephanie. But he also understood. Sheffield Memorial meant everything to her. She'd made the wrong decision for him, but the right one for the hospital. He wasn't sure what he would have decided in the same position. If he took the Mayo Clinic job he would have to make similar tough decisions.

Jason crossed and uncrossed his legs, uncomfortable in the visitor's chair across from Stephanie's empty desk. Despite the closed door, he could still hear the sounds of retching from her small private lavatory.

He winced with sympathy.

Finally he heard sounds of hand-washing and teeth-brushing.

Stephanie walked in to meet him, all poise and grace, as if she *hadn't* been heaving for the last ten minutes. She unwrapped a mint from her cut-crystal bowl, popped it in her mouth and sat, straight-spined and direct-eyed, if a little pale, ready to get on with their meeting.

Despite his best intentions, he felt himself soften

around the edges at her bravado. "Stephanie, is this morning sickness or a real illness?"

She gave him a baleful stare. "From where I'm sitting, this morning sickness feels pretty real to me."

"You're past the first trimester. It should be subsiding by now. Shouldn't you do something about it?"

"Do you think I'd be doing it if I could stop it?" She glared at him as if her morning sickness was all his fault.

He guessed in a way it was. Maybe his remarks had been a bit insensitive to a hormonal woman. But then, violently emptying one's stomach every morning would put anyone in a bad mood.

"Sorry." He reached for a mint. "I'm feeling a bit queasy myself."

"Couvade Syndrome." She put on her glasses—the ones that always turned him on. Maybe sex was the reason he couldn't clamp down on his reactions to her.

No, he had to face it. Even with her face pale and smudges under her eyes he felt—he felt tenderness for the mother of his child. The emotion was enough of a distraction that his brain refused to supply him with the particulars of the medical condition Couvade Syndrome.

Just another proof that, for him, medicine and emotion didn't mix.

"This patient has Couvade Syndrome?" He brought the conversation back to business.

"No, you do." Now her eyes twinkled, despite the dark circles under them. "It's a documented psychological condition that some men get when women are pregnant. Most people call them sympathy pains. Expect weight gain, excessive hunger and occasional bouts of morning sickness." She pointed to the pot of hot water boiling in an electric kettle on her credenza. "Why don't you pour both of us a cup of ginger tea?"

Jason's first inclination was to deny any kind of psycho-physical reaction to her pregnancy but he swallowed down his protest. Instead, he jumped to comply with her request for tea. Anything to ease the discomfort of carrying his child.

That was when Stephanie caught a glimpse of his clipboard on the floor next to his chair. The coversheet lay askew, and she could just make out the document on top with the Mayo Clinic letterhead. It could be anything—research paper, grant application…employment offer? The little she could see of the document looked very similar to the recruiting documents she was mailing out herself.

But Jason would discuss his future plans with her, wouldn't he?

Why should he? Her conscience nudged. What had she done to encourage that kind of sharing?

Was it too late? She had to try. For her own sake as well as her baby's.

Wanting to feel that electric touch of his, she let her fingertips brush his knuckles as he gave her the cup. Maybe it was hormonal overreaction, but she would swear the spark was hotter than ever between them. "Thank you."

Jason frowned as he took his seat and deliberately looked at his watch.

"The case?" he prompted, his voice as bland as if there had never been anything between them.

To keep her emotions in check, she concentrated on being professional. "Amelia Barker, aged sixteen. She's been diagnosed as being bulimic, but her psychologist wants to rule out any physical problems as part of his rudimentary diagnosis."

"Wouldn't Dr. Phillips be better suited for this one?"

"Dr. Phillips is putting together her first grant package. Her deadline is looming and she's running behind. And before you suggest him, Dr. Riser is spending more time in cardio until our workload picks up. So that leaves you and me."

"I'm a physician—from the word *physical*. I use physical evidence to diagnose problems. Tests— like the DNA samplings for Maggie." He pointed to the clipboard in his lap.

Was that what the paperwork from the Mayo Clinic was? Information on Maggie's case?

Agh! Her moods were swinging faster than she could keep up with them. She had to stay in control here. She had a department to run. *Professionalism*, she told herself. "Amelia's social worker is connected to me through one of the Sheffield-Montclair charity foundations. I said Diagnostics would take care of her exam. It's not like we're overloaded."

"I don't do head-games—especially teenaged girls' head-games."

Stephanie took off her glasses and rubbed circles into her temples. "Jason, I promised."

"Headache? Want me to take care of it? I could take down your hair and massage away the tension."

How could he act so caring, yet so cavalier at the same time? She just knew that when he looked at her with that protective possessiveness in his eyes she felt very, very safe and secure. She had the strongest urge to feel his arms wrapped around her.

That would really blur the line between professional and personal behavior, wouldn't it?

Despite her hormones, she withstood temptation. "There are discrepancies in the diagnosis. Don't you want to take a look?" Stephanie shoved the folder across her desk within his easy reach, knowing he couldn't resist an unresolved case.

Curiosity warred with disinterest in his eyes. "Shouldn't the girl be treated as an outpatient? Why has she been admitted to Pediatrics."

"She's dehydrated. They've got her on fluids. They're talking about a feeding tube soon."

Jason narrowed his eyes. "Will I be the lead on this case or will you?"

They'd never had to define who was in charge before. They had worked together so well it hadn't mattered who was the primary physician. But she had obviously shattered their smoothly working relationship with the lawsuit settlement.

Under Jason's intense scrutiny, she felt as if she'd destroyed a sacred trust. "This is your case if you want it, Jason."

Without commitment, Jason picked up the folder and flipped it open. Within minutes he looked up at her. "This could be interesting."

His brilliance at absorbing and assimilating information always astounded her. Reading the girl's file would have taken her at least twice as long, and she would have had to refer to it several times to glean all the information he had garnered in only a few minutes.

"You don't think she has an eating disorder?"

He shrugged. "At this point I'm unbiased. I'd like to check out a few things before concurring. Let's go take a look."

Outside the observation room, Stephanie stopped Jason with a hand to his arm. "Wait a moment."

The skin-to-skin contact created tingles throughout her central nervous system.

She knew he felt it too when he looked pointedly at the place on his arm where she touched.

She jerked her hand away, as if breaking the connection could stop the sensations she felt standing this close to him, and forced her attention back to the girl. "Being a sixteen-year-old is hard enough, but Amelia is also in the foster care system."

Jason nodded. "I read that in her file."

"There's more beyond her file. The only reason we're seeing her now is because she's just been moved from a group care facility to private caregivers—an older couple. The couple think the social worker, state-appointed psychologist and the pediatrician are all wrong with the diagnosis of bulimia."

"So you think it may be a case of new foster parents wanting a pill to fix the problem instead of welcoming damaged goods into their home?"

"No, that's not what I meant—well, not that harshly, anyway. The couple seem to be very concerned about Amelia. Her foster mother says she has a sixth sense about these things. I don't want to discount her feelings, but…."

"But they're unsubstantiated feelings and not to be trusted? Feelings don't count?"

"That's not…." Stephanie looked to the ceiling for an answer, but found no help in the white tiles. "All I'm saying is you're the best doctor for this job."

"Because I have no feelings. Got it."

Did he say that with pride or with regret? She couldn't be sure, but thought she detected weariness in his voice.

"Jason." She wanted to smooth things over but wasn't sure how. "I'm not at my best with diplomacy today."

"Forget about it. Candy-coated words aren't one of my requirements."

"Thanks." She debated advising him on interview style, not wanting to insult him further by implying he needed her coaching, but then did it anyway. "Jason, teenaged girls are very sensitive—especially foster children with troubled pasts. Try to be more tactful with her than I was with you, okay?"

"I've never been a girl, but I've got experience in the other departments. I can handle this."

On that obscure statement, he turned away from her and pushed through the door, leaving her staring at his very broad back. Stephanie wished she could have seen if the look on his face revealed any more than the flat tone of his voice had. There was so much she didn't know about this man who had shared her bed.

Stephanie followed him in, watching Amelia's shoulders tighten as she braced herself for whatever was to come.

According to Amelia's history, change was the only constant in her life. What would it be like, being shuffled from place to place with no consistency at all?

Holding a grudge because her mother had missed her ballet recital when she was twelve felt rather petty in the face of Amelia's erratic home-life.

Jason took the visitor's chair next to the bed to be at eye level with Amelia. It was a technique he'd recommended to her when he'd first joined the Sheffield. "*No one likes to be talked down to—*

not even kids," he'd told her. She'd never thought about it before.

"I'm Dr. Drake and this is Dr. Montclair."

The girl gave him a fleeting sideways glance through her hair, then turned her attention to her hands, clasped in her lap.

"Why are you here, Amelia?"

"They're worried that I've lost weight," she mumbled.

Amelia had just given them the perfect opening to ask about self-induced vomiting. Stephanie moved closer to probe gently, but Jason sent her a cautionary look with the slightest head-shake.

She bit the inside of her cheek, keeping quiet as he wordlessly warned her off. Everything Jason did, he did for a reason. She trusted his methodology even when she doubted his bedside manner.

Jason took his stethoscope from around his neck. "We check the basics, like heart rate and lungs, ears, eyes, nose and mouth, on everyone who comes into Sheffield Memorial. Because we're a teaching hospital each doctor does his own exam, so Dr. Montclair will check behind me. Just be patient with us, okay?"

Amelia gave Stephanie a hard look. "Is she new?"

"Actually, she's my boss. You've got the top two physicians in the department taking care of you."

Instead of finding that information reassuring, Amelia became alarmed. "Why? What's wrong with me? Is it serious?"

Jason frowned, looking more grave and concerned than he usually did. "I don't know yet. That's why we need to examine you."

Stephanie bit her lip, wishing Jason had said something more reassuring to the girl. This was where she usually jumped in, but Jason's body language was giving her every indication to stand back. This was his case and she would respect that.

"I'll listen to your lungs from your back and then from your chest, okay?" He held up the bell of his stethoscope and waited for permission.

Amelia shrugged. "Okay."

Still, she flinched as soon as he put his hand on her shoulder to steady her.

To the girl, Jason appeared not to notice. But he shot Stephanie a sharp, subtle look, making sure she'd caught Amelia's reaction. She gave him a discreet nod.

Working with Jason was like dancing, and this choreography was proving rather tricky.

No other doctors in her department worked as

smoothly together as they did. What would she do if he left her?

"Dr. Montclair, your turn," he said as he jotted notes in his file.

Stephanie listened, hearing a slight wheeze but a strong, steady heartbeat. She stepped back to write her own notes.

Jason held out his otoscope. "Could you hold your hair back, Amelia, so I can check your ears?"

Normally he would simply brush the hair back himself. Reluctantly, Amelia pulled back the limp brown strands to reveal a yellowish bruise fading on her neck—a bruise Jason must have noticed earlier.

This time he was very careful not to touch her as he checked her ears, then her eyes, nose and mouth, treating her cautiously, like a trauma case.

"Dr. Montclair will ask you a few questions while she examines you, okay? If you need me to step out so you can girl-talk, just let me know."

Stephanie picked up on her cue as she unpocketed her own otoscope. She did a cursory inspection of mouth and nose and eyes, then paused. "Amelia, I notice some bruising on your neck. What happened there?"

She bent to continue her inspection of Amelia's left ear, giving the girl a chance to talk without having to look at her. It was a technique that worked well for Stephanie, and one she tried to teach all the interns—another one she had learned from Jason.

She'd never realized until now how much she'd learned about her approach from Jason. Even though he wasn't much of a people person, he was a genius in technique when it came to approaching patients.

Why couldn't he do the same in personal relationships?

"It's not all about you, Stephanie." That was what her last serious boyfriend had said over a decade ago. But then she'd been finishing up medical school and the world had revolved around studying. She had brushed off his excuse as easily as she had brushed off the break-up, too busy to notice that he'd extricated himself from her life. She hadn't thought about him in years.

Amelia's ear looked clear, although there was some scarring from past infections. Still, she hadn't answered Stephanie's question about the bruising yet.

As Stephanie walked around the exam table to inspect the other ear Jason said, "I'll step outside a moment so you two can talk."

"No!" burst from Amelia. "Stay."

Apparently the girl had formed a bond with Jason. It happened more often than not, but generally with smaller children. They could sense Jason's stability, his strength and safety. That was how she always defended him to the board when she addressed his many complaints.

Stephanie finished her exam of Amelia's ear and stood back, letting Jason have center stage.

"Tell me straight, Amelia. How did those bruises get on your neck? A make-out session that got out of hand?"

At his bluntness, Amelia looked him in the eye, a dare in her glare. "I got into a fight."

"At school?"

"No, at my group home. A few weeks ago. Some new girl wanted the bed by the window, but that's where I was sleeping, so we—" she looked down, her bravado failing her "—we fought."

Fighting over a place to sleep? It was a lifestyle Stephanie couldn't comprehend. "Surely your house mother would have taken care of the problem if you'd gone to her?"

Both Jason and Amelia looked at her as if she had just spoken Martian.

Jason gave her a patronizing smile. "It doesn't always work like that, Dr. Montclair." Turning back to Amelia, he asked, "Do you still have that problem?"

"Not now. Since I've been moved from the group home I have my own bedroom."

"Good for you." Jason sounded as if he were congratulating Amelia on winning the lottery.

Just as the girl showed the slightest signs of relaxing, Jason asked, "Amelia, are you doing anything to purposely make yourself lose weight? Using laxatives? Making yourself throw up?"

So much for diplomacy. Stephanie wanted to bounce her head against his to force tact upon him. But this was Jason's case and she trusted him— even if she had to remind herself she did.

Amelia lifted her head, a defiant spark in her eyes. "No. I've told them all I'm not, but they don't believe me."

"I believe you." Sincerity rang through Jason's answer.

"Why?" Amelia asked the question Stephanie wanted an answer to, also. "Why do you believe me?"

"Because your new foster mother believes you. She's got good instincts."

What was Jason doing? Was he placating the girl to put her at ease? No. That wasn't Jason's way.

"And because your body isn't telling me you're

bulimic. There are signs. For instance, when people vomit a lot the bile from their stomachs rots their teeth. Yours look fine. But you *are* too thin for your height."

She shrugged, noncommittal but with no animosity.

"Being too thin will make you more susceptible to illnesses. More colds, more viruses. You've been in the foster care system long enough to know you've got to accept responsibility for taking care of yourself, right?"

She nodded. Another non-verbal response, but still a response.

Stephanie had never thought about that before. At Amelia's age, she hadn't been worried about her own health. Her mother or father had always noticed if she had sniffles, or they'd insisted she get a few extra hours of sleep when she'd been studying too late.

Though she was still determined to find a better balance with her own child, she had to admit, in retrospect, her parents had been much more involved in her life than she'd given them credit for.

Jason flipped open Amelia's chart, even though Stephanie knew he had it memorized.

"I see you play basketball. Dr. Montclair did, too. What position, Amelia?"

"I started off as point guard, but ended up as small forward before the season ended."

"I can see where your height would come in handy at point guard." He glanced at Stephanie and she waited for her cue. "What position did you play, Dr. Montclair?"

Casual conversation to establish a rapport. Jason must be getting ready for some in-depth interview questions since he was trying to get Amelia to open up to both of them.

Specifically, what did Jason want her to bring into the conversation? Playing off his observation about Amelia's height, Stephanie deduced that Jason wanted a comment about positive self-image from her.

When she worked with Jason, there was something metaphysical about their relationship that made Stephanie's blood rush.

She didn't have to search hard for the remark Jason wanted. She had fond memories of her high school basketball days, so making a comment here was easy enough.

"Shooting guard and point guard. I was the tallest girl in school. It was nice to feel that my height gave me an advantage."

He rewarded her with a sincere smile that

warmed her to her toes. Why did his approval make her glow like an infatuated teenager?

"And you, Dr. Drake? What did you play?" Amelia asked, drawn out by his charisma, no doubt.

A ghost of sadness crossed his eyes. "I didn't play sports. I transferred schools a lot and didn't stay in one place long enough to be part of a team."

"Too bad. You would have been awesome."

There was the hero-worship his patients usually gave him. If he could only work that magic on their parents, Stephanie's job would be so much easier.

Again, the thought that he might be leaving Sheffield reverberated through her. No. He couldn't leave. He was too good a doctor and Sheffield needed him. *She needed him.*

Before she could talk herself out of that notion, Jason shot another question at Amelia.

From the edge in his voice, he was getting into hunter mode, tracking the signs to identify and obliterate his prey: Amelia's illness.

This was where he needed Stephanie to keep up the rapport while he did his interrogation. Classic good cop-bad cop. They'd run this play many times before. As long as Amelia didn't get alarmed at his intensity, as some of the parents had in the past, they should be successful.

"Amelia, your records indicate you've lost over twenty pounds since you were weighed in for the basketball team. Are these records accurate?"

"Mostly." The girl seemed to take his business tone in stride.

Stephanie smiled encouragingly and exuded acceptance of Amelia's answers while Jason probed deeper. Some day she'd like to switch roles and play the bad cop, but Jason played bad so well she didn't know if she'd ever have that chance. But then if he left the Sheffield she'd have to find another partner to play with anyway.

She found herself frowning—not part of her good cop role.

Her own inner angst had no place in this interview. She vowed to keep her personal life out of the examination and focus on the girl in front of her.

"Mostly?" Jason asked. His eyes were already growing flat as he ran possible diagnoses through his head.

"I lost some weight before that, too."

"When did you first notice?"

"Last summer."

"What did you do last summer? Go hiking? Go camping? Swim in a lake and swallow a gulp of the water?"

"No, none of that."

"Eat strange food from an exotic locale?"

Amelia grimaced. "We had an International Culture Day at this day camp I went to. We had all sorts of strange food there. Some of it was nasty, but nobody got sick."

"Contaminates don't always affect the whole food supply. You could have just gotten the unlucky serving. Or your immune system could have been compromised at the time—one of your frequent sinus infections, maybe?"

"Maybe. I get them so often I don't pay attention to them much."

"You've got to be aware of your own health, Amelia, and ask for help. That's how it works for all of us. We all need to ask for help on occasion."

Stephanie tried to remember the last time Jason had asked for anything, much less help. The doctor could use a dose of his own medicine there.

Jason made a notation, then asked, "Amelia, how's your appetite now?"

"I get hungry, but then I feel sick in my stomach at the same time." Amelia looked as if she expected the doctors to doubt her. "Does that make sense?"

"Yes, it does. Dr. Montclair is pregnant and has morning sickness. I imagine she experiences those same mixed feelings—don't you, Dr. Montclair."

So much for keeping her personal life personal. "Yes, I do, Dr. Drake."

"I'm not pregnant," Amelia said.

"Your urine sample verifies that," Jason concurred. "How about gas?"

Amelia hid herself behind her hair to answer. "Yes, sometimes."

"How often is sometimes?"

"Almost always after I eat."

"And diarrhea?"

Amelia blushed bright red. "Yes," she whispered.

Remembering the sensitivity of her teen years, Stephanie felt for her.

But Jason didn't seem to notice. His eyes glittered with the light that said he was closing in on the problem. "We'll need a fresh stool sample."

Amelia visibly shrank away from him.

"It's important so we can find out how to make you better," Stephanie tried to reassure her. "You'll have plenty of privacy."

"I need to palpate your abdomen, Amelia."

Stephanie interpreted. "If you would please lie down, Dr. Drake is going to press your stomach to see if he feels anything swollen or hard. You must tell him if it feels numb or sore, okay?"

"Okay."

Jason gave Stephanie a grateful smile as he donned a pair of latex gloves.

Yes, they had great synchronicity.

Stephanie helped Amelia lie back, then put on her own gloves so she could follow Jason's probing hands with her own.

After a command to take deep breaths, Jason probed Amelia's abdomen, pausing over her liver. His eyes were unfocused as he used his hands to give him the answers he sought.

"Is this sore, Amelia?"

"A little."

Jason stood back. "Dr. Montclair, your turn."

Stephanie's fingertips found the nodules on Amelia's liver that had made Jason pause.

As soon as she was done Jason caught her eye, and she gave her nod of assent. She had felt an anomaly, too.

"Amelia, Dr. Montclair and I are going to compare notes, probably do a couple more tests, then come up with the best solution for you."

Jason didn't bother with a reassuring smile. That was one of the things the parents complained about. Jason always countered by saying he did what was best for his patients, not their parents.

"Is it bad?"

"I don't know yet." He looked the teen in the eyes. "But, whatever it is, I'll fix it."

"I believe you."

Just like that. In under twenty minutes Jason had engendered trust in a girl who didn't trust anyone.

Amelia wouldn't have believed a forced smile or a placating sentiment. But she believed Jason.

Yes, he was worth the trouble to try to keep.

CHAPTER NINE

"It's not bulimia," Jason said as soon as they were in Stephanie's office.

"I don't think so either."

"Skip the stool sample. I need a colonoscopy and liver biopsy."

"A colonoscopy? You are *not* going to be that girl's favorite doctor." She flipped open Amelia's chart. "You saw in Amelia's file that she has attachment issues. 'Avoids caregiver. Does not seek comfort or advice from caregiver. Unable or unwilling to share thoughts and feelings with others.' Since she's finally reached out for help, I would like to avoid as much discomfiture for her as possible. Why put her through an invasive procedure when a stool sample would do just as well?"

Jason was well aware of the variations of Attachment Theory. His own brother had been diagnosed the same as Amelia. Social Services was fond of labels.

As a child of six, he himself had been labeled

with 'Disorganized Attachment,' which meant he'd taken on the parental role for both his little brother and his own mother. That was the summer Social Services had removed him and his brother from his mother for the first time. Not everyone had an easy upbringing.

Jason wavered on the invasive testing, then his saner self prevailed. He couldn't let sympathy stop him from doing what was right. He only had to remember his little brother to know that.

"No. We can't do a thorough assessment without a colonoscopy. We could miss too much."

"Are you thinking giardiasis?"

"Doubtful. Amelia hasn't been near unclean water sources, which is the usual way to encounter giardiasis around here. But she was near food that could have been contaminated. I'm thinking amoebiasis caused by entamoeba histolytica. If it's far enough advanced she could have liver abscesses."

Stephanie bent a paperclip in two as she considered his hypothesis. "Ameobiasis isn't normal for our part of the world."

"Amelia became sick after she ate food at an International Culture Day." He loved the way she double-checked and challenged him. When she questioned him, she made his diagnoses stronger.

"The fever usually comes from secondary infections. When I worked at the free clinic I treated a family of missionaries who had been infected. The symptoms presented differently in each family member. In fact one of the missionaries had no symptoms but ended up being a carrier. If this does prove to be amoebiasis, we need to check everyone who ate the food that day."

"Colonoscopies all around. Won't that make for happy campers?"

Jason couldn't help but grin as he reached over and turned a page in Amelia's chart. Nobody could find a way to ease a situation quite like Stephanie. "The broad-spectrum antibiotics the health unit keeps prescribing for Amelia's sinus infections have helped to fight off other secondary infections that her weakened immune system might be susceptible to."

"That makes sense." She drummed her pen. "Our lab may be challenged, evaluating for entamoeba histolytica. I'll make sure they call the right people for advice."

"Page me when the results are in." Jason checked his watch. "I'm heading downstairs to observe Maggie's physical therapy session."

"Problems?"

"Maggie's therapist says Maggie has been reluctant to crawl. She's already lost walking. I want to see for myself." Jason had a bad feeling that little Maggie wouldn't be one of his success stories.

"You're her best hope, Jason." Stephanie rested her hand on his.

He fought his initial inclination to pull away. This was Stephanie. Instead, he took a deep breath and accepted the warmth of her comfort. "Thanks."

Right now he needed her belief in him to keep going. Amelia's case had brought back too many memories he'd tried to forget a long time ago.

Stephanie put a rush on Amelia's test results, knowing her foster parents wanted her home to finish settling in as soon as possible. The results proved Jason right.

As she often did, Stephanie offered to talk to Amelia's guardians. As usual, Jason accepted her offer.

She enjoyed speaking with Amelia's foster parents, the Davisons. They were an older couple, and had been opening their homes and hearts to foster children for over three decades. They took in older children—the ones that no one else wanted to invest time with.

"All children need love," Amelia's foster mother said.

Stephanie couldn't imagine loving a teen, then watching that teen grow up and leave so quickly. "It takes someone with a special heart to be a foster parent."

"We don't feel complete unless there's a child in our house to care for. We weren't blessed with biological children, and we're sure the reason is because taking in foster children is what we were made to do. It's a calling—like being a doctor. We would be living only half a life if we didn't fulfill our purpose."

Stephanie heard the passion in Mrs. Davison's voice. She'd heard that same passion in many doctors' voices—including Jason's. She was sure it was in hers, too.

After her consultation with the foster parents, she was surprised to find Jason in Amelia's room, explaining her condition to her.

"You're going to feel worse before you feel better, as the protozoa die off and your liver abscess heals," Jason finished up, "but you can handle it. Just take it easy, and in a few weeks you'll be fine. Be sure to let your foster parents know if you notice any of the symptoms we discussed. They're good folks. Give them a chance."

Stephanie knocked on the open doorway. "Amelia, how are you feeling?"

"Very clean inside."

Stephanie laughed. She'd been warned by the technicians that she'd have a very surly teenager on her hands, but it seemed Jason had cajoled Amelia into a better mood.

Jason stood to leave. "Remember what I said."

"I will," Amelia promised.

As Jason's shoulder brushed hers Stephanie had to concentrate on what she was about to say. She had an immediate yearning for a kiss from him. Hormones, no doubt.

"Your foster parents are on their way." Stephanie smiled at the girl. "I've talked to them about your condition and your medication and they are fully prepared to take care of you."

"Jason? Jason Drake?" Mr. Davison said from the hallway.

Stephanie turned in time to see the man clap Jason on the shoulder while his wife gave him a bear hug.

"It's been a long time," she heard Jason say.

"Look at you—a big-time doctor. As smart as you are, that fits. He was always looking after the little ones—remember, Helen?"

"I remember. I know two people who will be so glad we ran into you. Tell us how to contact you."

Stephanie knew she shouldn't be eavesdropping, but she couldn't make herself stop.

Jason pulled a card from his pocket and scribbled on it. "Here's my cell phone number. Call me."

Less than a half-dozen people had Jason's personal cell number. He never gave it to anyone.

"We will, Jason. We will."

"It's so good to see you." This time Mr. Davison hugged him. Jason amazed Stephanie by hugging back.

"We'll be calling you soon."

"I hope so." Without even looking back at Stephanie, he left.

Stephanie stared at the back of the man she knew less and less.

They'd never talked about his life before the hospital. At first she hadn't wanted to. Theirs was supposed to be an uncomplicated arrangement with no strings attached.

When it had become more—at least more to her—she vaguely remembered leading up to asking, but he'd always diverted her. Usually with a slow, deep kiss that had made her forget everything but satisfying her body's craving for him.

She had always thought she had time.

But now she could lose Jason and she would

never know the man he was inside. She had to find a way to convince him to stay.

Mrs. Davison lightly touched her on the shoulder. "Dr. Montclair, could we get through the doorway? We'd like to see our girl."

Stephanie used all her will-power to stay professional and refrain from begging the couple to tell her everything they knew about Jason.

She would ask him herself. And she wouldn't let herself be diverted this time—despite her hormone-influenced libido.

After waiting for the perfect opportunity, Stephanie finally realized she would have to force the issue. But how? How did she get Jason to talk to her when for the last few weeks he'd acted as if she was part of the scenery?

The Renovation Committee's budget meeting was running late into the evening and Stephanie's stomach growled.

They had been discussing a bronze of her grandfather for the remodeled entrance hall for the last forty-five minutes. Remembering her grandfather, Stephanie was sure he would have preferred the money go to a scholarship fund for promising medical students, but one of the committee members had a friend who did bronze sculptures. As she was an ad hoc member of the committee she didn't get a vote, but she would be drafting a letter in the morning.

Tonight all she wanted was pizza. In fact if she didn't get a thin crust pizza with bell peppers and pepperoni she would likely tear someone's head off.

Pizza and Jason, a quiet voice deep inside insisted. Two overpowering needs. The mystery of Jason had been heavy in her thoughts ever since Amelia's exam. His unknown past intrigued her, but his future—their future—made her yearn for him with a hunger that far surpassed pizza.

If she could only discover how to grow their relationship while she grew their baby, maybe they could be a family in some form or fashion.

Understanding and communication was where their relationship broke down. But she would do everything she could to change that. And she was certain that understanding Jason's past was essential to understanding the man he was today.

Stephanie twitched in her seat as Dr. Wilkins blathered on. Tomorrow was a big day: her first ultrasound. She would see her baby. That would make the whole pregnancy real to her in a way it hadn't been before. While reading through some résumés before the meeting she'd felt her baby quicken. Not gas, but the tiniest little flutter. She was sure of it.

She was growing a tiny life inside her. Talking about bronze busts sounded so trivial beside the miracle of life.

She gathered her scattered thoughts and stood. "Gentlemen..." she looked around at the all-male room "...we are now talking in circles. Let's meet again this time next week and see if we can move forward."

After they'd received her letter of recommendation. This was office politics. She'd learned it at her mother's knee. Listen politely and respectfully, then be diplomatic, yet practical.

As she was slated to step into her father's shoes when he retired from the board, she needed to keep her finger on the pulse of the whole hospital, not just her little corner of it in Diagnostics.

Business over with, she called in her pizza order for pick-up, but the thought of eating alone dampened her appetite.

On impulse, she upgraded from a small pizza to a large one. She'd never been to Jason's home, so she looked up his address in her personnel file.

Of course she was working off the hope that he would be there. She didn't really know what Jason did in those rare hours he spent away from work.

He'd used to spend them with her, until she broke up with him.

There was so much between them now. The break-up, the lawsuit, the baby.

Would he see the pizza as a peace offering and at least be willing to discuss the baby? Would he even be home?

It was a chance she was willing to take as she drove toward the outskirts of town.

She had caught a glimpse of deep emotion, a crack in his heretofore impenetrable surface, when he'd spoken with Amelia. And then the hugs in the hallway with Amelia's foster parents—a spontaneous show of affection she would have never expected from him.

How much of this man had she never seen before because she'd pushed him away? The passion was still there between them. Could they build on that?

She owed it to herself and to her baby—and to Jason—to try.

Passing through the suburbs, she took a look at the residential houses and wondered about the families inside.

Her own condominium was perfect for one busy doctor, but it didn't have a yard for a flowerbed or a sidewalk for a stroller or a tricycle. Maybe she should think of moving.

Did Jason already have a home perfect for a family—their family? With a start, she realized she'd worked Jason into her daydreams.

What would Jason's home reveal about him?

Her home said that she had money to hire an expensive decorator who knew how to strategically place heirlooms to their best advantage. The only detail she had insisted upon had been the collection of small framed family portraits on the mantel. She liked seeing all her stalwart ancestors staring down at her, reminding her of the continuity of life.

But what about Jason? She'd never even heard him mention family before. Would he have told her more if she had asked?

Keeping up the illusion of a summer fling, she had acted as if they only lived for the moment. As if their pasts and futures didn't matter. They mattered now.

The closer she got to Jason's house, the older the neighborhood became. His duplex and the two on either side of him looked like daisies among a stand of weeds, with their fresh paint and neatly trimmed yards.

The house was dark. She checked the address. This was the right place but Jason wasn't here.

Was he really leaving Sheffield? Leaving her

and their baby? She tried to put that worry from her mind daily, but hadn't managed to stave it off.

Her stomach clenched to the point of pain, but she doubted it was from hunger.

Should she wait for him?

She had always hated waiting. Maybe it was time she learned patience.

She could sit right here, eat her pizza and wait.

She had picked the pepperoni off one piece of pizza, cleaned out all the old voicemail messages on her phone and was flipping through heretofore unexplored channels on her radio when she heard the roar of Jason's motorcycle.

He wheeled in behind her, looking dangerous in jeans and T-shirt, helmet covering his face. She'd always had a thing for men on motorcycles, even in her teens. Her heart raced as she remembered her rescue ride on the back of the bike the night of the fundraiser. It was an experience she would like to repeat—without the humiliating speech preceding it, of course.

Jason parked his bike, took off his helmet and pulled open her car door. "Stephanie?"

"I've brought supper. You haven't eaten yet, have you?"

Jason took the pizza box she held out to him, then

offered his other hand to help her out of her car. He looked different here. Vulnerable. Confused.

She liked that. She liked being the woman who could knock the stoic Dr. Drake off-balance. He certainly did the same to her.

"Jason, would you like to eat out here in the driveway or inside your house?"

He blinked, as if he'd just awakened from a dream, then cupped her elbow to guide her into his house. "Is everything all right?"

"No, it's not."

That stopped him in his tracks. "What's wrong?"

She was pleased to note that his voice held the slightest hint of alarm, instead of that flat, unemotional tone he usually employed for emergencies. But she didn't let him worry too long.

"I'm having my first craving, and I'm not going to have it alone. Since you shared in the making of this baby, it's only right you share in its feeding, too."

Right at this particularly euphoric moment Stephanie wasn't sure why she had ever thought to exclude Jason from her life and the life of their child. But what if she had succeeded in pushing him away? Almost as a compulsion, she reached out for him, put her hand on his chest, touched his warmth through his thin T-shirt, felt the pounding of his heart and the rise and fall of his chest.

And knew they were bound together by more than the child she carried.

Now to convince Jason of that.

They might have stood there all night, but a car down the block backfired. Jason broke contact, putting himself between her and the street, protecting her.

"Let's get inside." He opened the door of his house to a neat, clean and comfortable living room. He had a huge television, two equally huge brown leather recliners, a matching couch and a coffee table. The galley kitchen was barely big enough for one to fit comfortably and it was spotless.

If Stephanie had had to imagine a typical bachelor pad, this would be it. Except for the large pile of parenting books Jason had stacked beside one of the recliners.

"No dining table." He shrugged apologetically. "I usually eat in front of the TV. Have a seat."

He put the pizza down on the coffee table and retrieved two plain white plates from a cabinet.

Stephanie chose the couch. They'd always sat on the couch in her living room, purposely letting their knees bump. Would he sit next to her tonight?

Jason brought two folded paper towels for napkins and two glasses of apple juice.

"Thanks." As soon as she scooped up the first slice of pizza Jason's phone rang.

No, not Jason's phone. The E.R. on-call phone. He munched while he talked, reassuring whoever was on the other end that they had followed the correct procedures and made the right call in admitting a possible heart attack patient for a workup.

As he finished the call and took a seat on the couch next to her he lifted an eyebrow, half-apologetic, but also half-challenging.

"I'm trying to handle on-call for Mike tonight," he explained. "One of his kids has a school play. The E.R. has a new doctor on duty who's a bit nervous, so we might get interrupted again."

"It's okay," Stephanie reassured him. And it really was. Jason had a calling and he had to answer it.

"That's not what I was expecting from you. Who are you and what did you do with Stephanie?"

"That's who doctors are. That's who you are and that's who I am." Communication. If she expected him to talk to her, she had to be open with him. She took a deep breath. "What I'm not is a diversion until an intriguing medical challenge comes along. I want to feel wanted, to feel needed—to feel important to your world."

"You always seem so self-sufficient, so sure of yourself. Like you dare anyone to insult you by thinking you might be so inept as to need anyone."

"That stings."

"It wasn't meant to." He gave her a lopsided grin. "I thought you might take it as a compliment."

"I think it was the sting of truth." She leaned back against the couch. "I've spent all my life trying to prove to myself that I don't need anyone. Instead I convinced everyone else."

Communication. It really did go both ways.

Feeling emboldened, she reached for Jason's hand and put his palm on her stomach. "I felt the baby today."

"Really?" His eyes showed a mixture of excitement and concern. His large hand hovered over her rounded abdomen until she gave him a reassuring nod. "Isn't it too early?"

"I might be feeling fetal movement, or I might be feeling normal uterine contractions. Either way, it's because our baby is in there."

"Do you feel anything now?"

"Not now. But I think I did a few minutes ago." She watched his face as he splayed his fingers, trying to ascertain any movement through the material of her dress. "It's so subtle. I have to be very still and quiet."

Reverently he closed his eyes and held his breath.

Then his cell phone rang again.

They both jumped as if they'd been caught kissing behind the barn. Reluctantly Jason removed his hand and grabbed the phone. Stephanie grabbed another piece of pizza.

While Jason was on the phone, his doorbell rang.

"Would you get that for me, please, Stephanie?"

The young man at the door was Jason's next door neighbor and tenant, who had come over to pay the rent. She learned that Jason owned several well-maintained houses on either side of them. He rented exclusively to struggling medical students. The monthly stipend Jason requested was paltry— and he frequently waived it at the first of each semester, when university fees were due.

His generosity was as great or greater than those who wrote checks for her fundraisers. But Jason gave his time as well as his money, fixing faulty plumbing and holding tutoring sessions before finals.

What else about this man did she not know?

After the phone call Jason finished off three pieces of pizza while she made him laugh at the posturings of the Renovations Committee. She'd missed that rare smile of his.

Impulsively, she said, "I've got my first ultrasound scheduled for tomorrow afternoon. If you want to drop in and take a peek you're welcome to."

She hadn't planned to invite him. It had just happened.

And, being honest with herself, she really wanted someone to share her joy.

Not just someone. Jason.

She wanted to see the look on his face when he heard his baby's heartbeat and saw it move within her.

He sat back on the couch as if he'd just been sucker punched. She watched the muscles in his throat convulse.

"I *would* like that, Stephanie. Thank you." His voice sounded gruff. "When and where?"

"At two in Dr. Sim's office. Can you make it?"

"Yes. I'll be there."

Stephanie didn't let the warm fuzzy feeling spread through her at his words, even though she wanted to. She knew what he meant. *I'll be there if nothing else comes up.* He was a doctor after all.

"Don't make promises you can't keep." Her self-protective words were out before she could call them back. But a lifetime of expectation followed by disappointment couldn't be completely changed in a single day. She softened her response. "I know you'll do your best."

Then the cell phone rang again.

After another bout of instructions Jason returned to the couch, but didn't bother to sit. "I need to go in."

He had that mask on again—the one that hid the hurt. His jawline and shoulders were tight and square—braced for her rebuff, no doubt.

"I understand." She thought of all the times she'd castigated him for leaving. "All I need to know is that I'm not out of sight, out of mind. I'm not asking for you to choose between me and medicine. Just that we find some kind of balance."

"Life would have been a lot easier if you'd had this revelation earlier."

"I think this baby is making me grow up a bit." She laughed to cover her uncomfortable confession. "Some day soon I'd like to know about your upbringing."

He brushed it off. "Not much to tell."

Then his look grew sultry up and down the length of her, pausing on her abundant cleavage. "You look plenty grown up to me." His voice rasped, making her shiver with desire.

That was what he did any time the conversation started to get deeply personal: diverted with a remark that he knew would make her sizzle.

"I really would like to know what's behind the man you are."

He locked up behind them, then walked her to her car, trailing his hand down her spine. "Since your place is on the way, I'll follow you to make sure you get there okay."

"No need." Only a little closer to learning more about her baby's daddy, and now burning for his touch, she covered her frustration with a social smile. "I can find my own way home. See you tomorrow."

"There's that self-sufficiency again." He strapped on his helmet, ending her protests. "I'll follow you."

Knowing he was near *did* make her feel safer. "Thank you. I'd like that."

As she drove home, she couldn't help herself from looking back in her rearview mirror more often than usual to catch a glimpse of him.

That was *not* how her life would be—looking backward, wondering what she'd left behind.

She would fight for him, for herself and her baby.

CHAPTER TEN

STEPHANIE awoke with an energy she hadn't felt in over three months, and made it through the whole morning with no sign of sickness.

Now, almost noon, she was feeling great. She breathed in the scent of Jason's soap as he hovered, looking over her shoulder at the résumés on her desk. She had invited him in as Senior Fellow to make recommendations for their replacement doctor.

Jason sipped strongly caffeinated coffee, looking none the worse for wear after being up most of the night in the E.R., talking the new doctor through his first night jitters. Despite complaints that Jason was cold-hearted and rude, he was the first person anyone at Sheffield called when they wanted a level head. How could they not see the person behind the stoic façade? But, then again, she'd been guilty of the same thing.

Casually, almost absently, Jason rested his hands on her shoulders and began to massage away the tension at the base of her neck with his thumbs. She didn't even try to hold back the rapturous sigh that escaped.

This was how it had all started that first night she'd taken him home.

A cleared throat in the doorway broke the intimate moment. Dr. Phillips said, "Sorry to interrupt, but we have a teleconference at two o'clock on the new procedure you've been wanting to research, Dr. Drake. If we participate we can add our names to the list to be considered for a trial study the Mayo Clinic is sponsoring and our application will be complete. Sorry for the short notice. I'm running a bit behind on this one."

Dr. Phillips thrust documents in front of them that showed the time for the teleconference and the phone number for the sign-up list signatures to be faxed in before the conference began.

"Here's your copies." She handed the papers to Jason.

Stephanie held her breath, bracing herself for the pain that would accompany hearing Jason changing their plans.

Jason shook his head, no. "I'm busy at two, Dr. Phillips."

"But this is our only chance. We can only add a half-dozen names. I've got the Sheffield doctors with the best credentials signed up, but we really need your name on the list, too, Dr. Drake. Your success with last year's study will make us the obvious choice for getting this one if you'll sign up and attend. Tell him, Dr. Montclair—it's for the good of the hospital."

Stephanie could make this easy for him. She could exercise her authority and leave him with no choice but to sign up. She could tell him it didn't matter that he would miss the ultrasound. But it did matter.

"That's up to Dr. Drake."

They both looked to Jason for his answer.

"Not this time, Dr. Phillips. I've got family commitments." Jason took a sip of coffee, rolled the liquid around in his mouth, then set the cup back on Stephanie's desk, each movement deliberate and controlled. "Ask Dr. Riser. He's got good credentials in this area, too."

Dr. Phillips studied him as if he were an unnamed virus strain under the microscope. "Okay, I'll ask him. But you're the right doctor for this project."

"There will be other projects."

"This doesn't have anything to do with that trumped-up lawsuit settlement, does it?"

"No. It's completely personal."

She looked from Jason to Stephanie, then back again to Jason. "It's none of my business, but—"

"You're right. It's not." He pointed to the the hot plate and the coffeepot Stephanie had provided when she'd invited him to her office. "Would you like to stay for a cup, or would you like to track down Dr. Riser before two o'clock? He was on his way to Cardio the last time I saw him."

"I hope you don't regret this later." On those parting words, Dr. Phillips turned and left.

Once she was gone, Stephanie stood, slipping her shoes back onto her feet. "I hope you don't regret it, either."

"I'm going to see my child for the first time. What could compare to that?"

A spark of hope ignited deep inside Stephanie. A spark that in the past she had snuffed out before it could grow. Could this really work? Could they really have a lasting relationship?

She caught a glimpse of longing in Jason's eyes as he read through the documents Dr. Phillips had left.

Cautiously, she banked that spark—not distinguishing it, but not letting it flame any brighter, either.

* * *

Jason cut short his phone consultation with Mount Sinai Medical Center's leading expert on chromosomal abnormalities as the clock ticked toward two o'clock. He wanted to ask more about the characteristics associated with the tip of the twenty-second chromosome, but that would have to wait. Still, he was confident he was on the right track with Maggie.

In the hallway, Dr. Riser brushed past him. "Excuse me. I'm in a bit of a rush. I've got a teleconference to get to. Trial study, you know? I would encourage you to attend, but it's by exclusive invitation only."

Jason shrugged. "Maybe next time."

Taking the stairs two at a time, he climbed the six floors from his office in the Diagnostics wing to the Obstetrics floor. He had intended to use the physical activity and private time to think about how to get Dr. Riser out of his department. Instead, all he could think of was how very complex and fragile was the development of a human, and how many things could go wrong. From gene mutations at conception to *in utero* complications, and plain old bad luck.

Once on the OB floor, he scanned the directory on the wall for the private offices of Dr. Sim. He rarely came up to this floor—had had no reason to until now. Dr. Sim was in the newer section of Montclair Tower, which was connected via a cross-walk between the two buildings.

He glanced at his watch. One minute until two. He'd cut it too close. But the geneticist he'd needed to speak to had been out of the country and un-available until now, so he'd had to—

He had to start learning to schedule better.

In the crosswalk, he jumped on the moving walk-way, weaving past those who leisurely stood and gazed out the glass windows at the traffic below. Why couldn't they all follow directions and stand to the right, to let faster moving traffic like him pass on the left?

Then the automated walkway made a grinding noise and stopped. Not waiting to see if it would start up again, he vaulted over the handrail and took off at a fast lope.

At a near-trot, he almost passed Dr. Sim's office, but rounded the corner just as the minute hand on his watch clicked to two minutes past two.

Skidding to a stop at Dr. Sim's receptionist center, he asked the attendant, "Where's Dr. Montclair?"

"Are you consulting, Dr. Drake?"

"No, I'm here as Dr. Montclair's—" What was he to her? "I'm here for Stephanie Montclair."

"Wait here, please."

"She's expecting me." He tried to push past her.

She put out her hand to stop him. "Privacy laws and respect for the patient. I'll run back and ask permission."

Jason gritted his teeth. It seemed all he did nowadays was ask Stephanie's permission.

He thought about the career possibilities that had been discussed with him at the Mayo clinic. His own research department and staff sounded like a dream come true.

But that would mean moving away from his child. And Stephanie.

Would she care?

Before yesterday evening he would have said no. She wanted more and he didn't have more—didn't even have a clue what more was.

"Dr. Montclair says you may come back, Dr. Drake." The attendant led the way to the ultrasound lab.

He gave a quick knock on the door and faintly heard, "Come in."

Stephanie lay on the examination table, wearing a faded blue-gray hospital gown and draped in a blue paper cloth. He'd seen hundreds of patients in similar situations, and the sight always started his brain on a logical diagnostic path.

But seeing Stephanie like this took all thought away. She leaned up on her elbows. "You came."

She sounded surprised. Relieved? Maybe.

"Of course I came."

Behind him, the ultrasound technician came in, followed by Dr. Sim. A room full of females. He usually didn't notice things like that.

Dr. Sim acknowledged him with a noncommittal nod of her head. "Dr. Drake."

He definitely felt like the odd man out. As he'd felt all his life before he graduated medical school.

In his own research lab he would never feel that way.

"Now, let's see if we can figure out why you were spotting, Stephanie."

He stepped up next to Stephanie, close enough so she could reach out and hold his hand if she wanted to. "I didn't know that was a problem."

Dr. Sim cocked an eyebrow at Stephanie, looking for her permission to fill him in.

Stephanie gave him a weak smile before she explained, "It's not a problem, but it is outside the norm. So we're checking it out today."

The technician stepped forward and squirted the ultrasound gel on Stephanie's belly, then angled the monitor so they could all see it.

Jason found himself lacing his fingers between Stephanie's. Her grip tightened, locking him in place.

As the technician ran the probe across Stephanie's slightly distended belly a grainy picture emerged on the screen.

Jason had done the minimum in obstetrics years ago as a resident, but hadn't had a case where he'd had to study it further since then—except for the quick cramming he'd done when Stephanie had told him about the ultrasound this morning.

And there it was. His child. A living, breathing part of him.

Stephanie looked up at him. "I didn't expect to feel…." Tears tracked down her face. "Look, Jason. Our baby is so…."

He didn't have the words either. Instead he wiped away her tears with his thumb, then on instinct followed with his lips.

A lump of tenderness rose in his throat, followed by a huge mass of protectiveness in his heart.

It was this kind of emotion that made a doctor miss important signs and symptoms. He worked hard to get himself under control, even though the warmth of Stephanie's hand distracted him.

He swallowed twice before he could speak.

"What are you looking for?" From his perspective, everything looked okay. Or maybe not. What was that shadow by the heart?

Dr. Sim frowned as she studied the monitor. "I don't see anything out of the norm." She used a pen to draw attention to the monitor.

"Phalanges are developed. Organs are all present. Tail is gone. Your baby is being modest. I can't tell the gender, although it's very difficult to determine with any certainty at this stage, anyway. Everything looks good here."

Jason moved as close as he could to the monitor without releasing Stephanie's hand. The shadow was gone—just an artifact on the monitor. In his mind, he ran through the list of tests Dr. Sim had most likely run at this early stage.

"How are her HCG levels?"

"Fine. All her bloodwork looks good."

"Physical examination?"

"Elevated blood pressure, but not dangerously high. At this point it's purely a concern and not an issue."

"Weight gain?"

"Right on schedule." Dr. Sim took another look at the monitor. "I think we've seen everything we need to see. Would you like a print of the ultrasound? Your baby's first photo, right?"

"Yes, I would." Stephanie started crying again.

"It's like I've sprung a leak." She dropped Jason's hand to accept the tissue Dr. Sim handed her.

"Is that a problem?" Jason realized he sounded more like a worried layman than an experienced doctor, but he hadn't read anything about excessive crying as he'd skimmed over his research material in the last few days.

If he hadn't had to attend that sensitivity training he would be up-to-date right now.

Dr. Sim smiled at them both. "Extreme emotional swings are perfectly normal at this stage of pregnancy. Your hormone levels are at their highest right now."

Jason patted Stephanie's hand. How hard must it be to manage a chemical reaction in your body so strong that it controlled your emotional state? All the men he knew would need a nice, quiet place to hibernate for nine months. Yet women thought beyond their emotional state, fulfilling all their obligations and in general, living life. Women were so strong that way.

Dr. Sim interrupted his thoughts. "Dr. Drake, if you would accompany me to my office, I'd like to get a family history from you. Dr. Montclair, after you dress I'd like you to join us, too."

Jason nodded. He hadn't even thought about

what he'd brought to this pregnancy beyond putting a baby in Stephanie's uterus.

But of course he carried his whole murky gene pool with him, and now he'd passed it on to their child just like Stephanie had hers.

Their child. One father. One mother. One child.

And together the three of them made up a family. The concept sent a shiver down his spine and raised the hairs on his arms.

Miraculous? Yes.

Scary? Hell, yes.

He pushed his emotional reaction to the side.

To care for his family, Dr. Sim would need to be aware of any inheritable defects.

Once again Jason would fail Stephanie. The information he had was incomplete. But he would do the best he could. It was what a man did for his family.

Maybe, if he hurried, he wouldn't have to confess his family defects in front of Stephanie. She could read about them in the report, but he wouldn't have to look her in the eye as he revealed all.

Stephanie hated that she had to find out about the father of her child from a medical history.

That was one of the many things wrong with this

relationship. But holding Jason's hand as they both saw the first image of their baby had felt so right.

Every baby needed a father. *And I need Jason.* She didn't want to think it. She didn't want to mean it. But she couldn't make it go away.

She needed Jason to hold her hand. To wipe her tears. To share their child's life.

To share *her* life.

Forever.

She longed for a future where she would feel Jason's arms around her, his breath on her neck, his whispers in her ear as they lay in bed together, nestled like two spoons in a drawer, night after night. Maybe it was her highly emotional state, but she yearned with an intensity that was painful.

She wanted him in every way a woman could want a man.

Her breasts ached. What would his hands feel like, cupping their newfound fullness? What would his lips feel like, kissing the sensitive tips? What would her womb feel like in joyous orgasm as he told her how beautiful she was and how much he loved her.

Did he love her?

She didn't know. And that was the crux of it.

Would she ever hear those words from him?

Could she ever say them aloud to him?

She wanted him in her heart, as well as in her head and in her body.

But wanting and having were two different things. To have Jason in her life she would have to give of herself. Was she willing to give herself to him? To trust him to be there for her? To forgive him when he failed?

That was if Jason would let her.

"If you don't mind, Dr. Sim, I would really appreciate having a moment with Jason alone."

"Of course. Take your time. I need to consult with my nurses anyway. Feel free to use my office if you'll be more comfortable." Dr. Sim smiled. "Dr. Drake, help yourself to a cup of coffee. I hear you had a long night in the emergency room. Must have been a full moon."

"Jason. Call me Jason." He turned his attention back to Stephanie. "I'll wait for you in Dr. Sim's office."

They started out the door together, leaving her alone. It had taken over five months before Jason had let *her* call him by his first name.

But she'd been a newly promoted department director and hadn't encouraged intimacy back then.

Three years. It had taken three years for her to realize she'd obtained all she'd aspired to and wanted more.

But *more* was supposed to have been a light romantic interest—not a full-blown love affair with a baby thrown into the mix.

Stripping off the frumpy wraparound gown, she reached for her own clothes.

Checking herself in the mirror, she felt pudgy even in an outfit chosen to look classically elegant. A strand of pearls, her new red ballet flats and the simple navy sheath that now only barely disguised her baby bump didn't make up for the bra that had begun to pinch, or the panties that rolled at the waistband.

Another few weeks and there would be no concealing her pregnancy. Not that she wanted to. Seeing her baby had made it more real than ever and she wanted to tell the world about it.

Aware of the sudden mood change over her body image, Stephanie was still unable to control it. She took a few extra seconds to pull her hair into a tight ponytail and to put a subtle coat of color on her lips—more for her own bolstering than for convention's sake.

The door to Dr. Sim's office stood open, with Jason waiting alone inside. He sat in a visitor's chair, reading her chart, learning all her medical secrets—not that she had any, other than her weight. She would have rather kept *that* number private.

Still, she felt naked, despite being fully dressed. Would she feel that way if they were in a committed relationship? Shouldn't she feel completely comfortable with Jason knowing everything about her?

Yet she knew little or nothing about Jason.

Jason was so engrossed in her chart that she slipped into the other visitor's chair before he even noticed her.

"See anything of interest?"

"Everything about you interests me, Stephanie. You're the mother of my child."

And to think that not too long ago she'd thought Jason would have no interest in parenthood. She had really misjudged him.

He was so hard to read. Then again, she was judging a book by its cover when she should be reading between the lines.

Stephanie picked up the clipboard with the questionnaire that sat on the corner of Dr. Sim's desk. "These are the questions Dr. Sim needs answers to. She wants yes or no answers. I want to hear it all."

"Why?"

"Everything about you interests me, Jason.

You're the father of my child," she paraphrased back to him.

Stephanie felt tension radiate from Jason. His hands clasped the arms of his chair and he sat forward, as if awaiting a jolt of electricity. Could his history be that bad?

"Let's get started, shall we?" She tried to keep her voice clinical, hoping that would ease his worry.

They began with the basics.

Jason's middle name was Alexander, and his birthday was a full eight months behind hers.

"I've always been attracted to older women," he quipped.

This was the dry humor Stephanie loved. It had completely disappeared after he'd learned of the baby. She was glad to see it back.

"Are there any inheritable diseases on your mother's or father's side?" She handed him a list with boxes to check. "Any history of high blood pressure? Diabetes? Cancer?"

Without even glancing at the paper, Jason handed it back to her. "I don't know. I've only seen my mother a handful of times in my life, and she wasn't in a state where I could analyze her physical health."

He cast a sideways glance at Stephanie, looked

away, then looked at her straight on. "There's mental illness on my mother's side, but it may be due to a chemical imbalance created by illegal drug and alcohol abuse rather than a genetic disposition."

His voice was quiet, steady, monotone—but his knuckles showed white where he gripped the chair-arm.

Those damned tears started to well again. She blinked them back. "Jason, I'm so sorry. Is she institutionalized?"

He shrugged—a casual gesture made so painfully guarded by his tension. "I was eighteen the last time I saw her. She was living on the street then."

Stephanie wanted to cover his hand with hers, but he looked so untouchable, so remote. She wasn't brave enough to violate that wall he'd erected around himself.

"Were you living with your father?"

"No. On my own."

Gently, Stephanie asked, "Do you know if your father has any health issues?"

"I never knew my father. My mother wasn't sure, either."

Stephanie thought of all the times she'd wished for a father more affectionate, more devoted, more in tune with her wants and needs. And Jason had only wished for a father he could name.

Stephanie wrote "*Unknown*" next to the question, as she had done with so many of them already. "Jason, do you have any siblings?"

"One brother. More than likely he was a half-brother." He said it reluctantly, as if having a brother was a bad thing. Maybe it had been, under the circumstances.

Stephanie had always wanted a brother or sister.

Was her own baby destined to be an only child? She'd never given it much thought, rationalizing that there was always time to worry about that later. But now, out of the blue, she had a longing for children. At least three. Maybe four.

"And his health?"

"He's deceased."

"I'm sorry to hear that." She barely got the words through her tear-clogged throat. "What did he die of?"

"Swelling of the brain from a sports injury. By the time I got him to the hospital he had lapsed into a coma. He never woke up."

Stephanie's heart ached at the pain in Jason's eyes, even while his voice held no emotion at all. "How old were you?"

"Eighteen. That's when I saw my mother. I put

the word out on the street and somehow she heard. She came for the funeral."

"But she didn't stay?"

"No. She never stayed." Jason clamped his lips tight, as if he could keep anything else from escaping.

"How old was your brother?"

"Fourteen."

"Do you have anyone else? Any other family?" she asked softly. "Anyone to contact in case of emergency?"

"No one else." Jason blinked, as if awakening from a trance.

No one other than her who cared if Jason lived or died. How lonely that must feel. She couldn't even imagine the depth of it.

Again, Jason did that uncanny thing he did, knowing her thoughts without her speaking them.

"There is one couple. I got their contact information from Amelia's foster parents. They were ministers who took in both my brother and me. We stayed there together for almost thirteen months. It was the longest I was ever in one place."

"Why did it end?"

"They were transferred to a different state. They wanted to adopt us—both of us—and take us with them. I was already fifteen by then, so it was a chance in a million with me being so old. But Social Services needed my mother's consent for release. She wouldn't let us go."

"Even though it would have been better for you?" Stephanie heard the heartache that had never healed despite the flatness of Jason's voice, although his face showed nothing—as if he were reading a case from a medical journal.

"She said she couldn't bear to give up her rights to her children—even though she hadn't seen us once in that whole time we'd been with the ministers. So we had to go back into the system. That's the last time my brother and I lived together until I turned eighteen and took custody of him." Jason took the paper from his pocket, looked at the contact information, then replaced the paper without entering it on the form. "That was years ago. They probably don't even remember me now."

Stephanie wanted to cover his hand, but was afraid she would break down at the slightest touch. Instead, she smiled through her tears. "I don't know about that, Jason Drake. You're pretty unforgettable."

In the doorway, Dr. Sim cleared her throat, drawing their attention. "I have the ultrasound prints."

She handed each of them a handful of black and

white images and a couple of small envelopes. "I'll email you the video."

"Thank you." Stephanie slipped hers into the envelope and tucked it inside her purse.

Jason scanned through the images, pausing on each one. His eyes glistened as he finally stacked them, tucked them into their envelope and reverently put them into his breast pocket. "Thanks."

"You're welcome." Dr. Sim retrieved the chart and looked over the scanty information.

"I don't have much of a history to give you, do I, Dr. Sim?"

"We all do the best we can with what we have." She put down her pen. "And may I say you've done very well?"

Jason ducked his head, as if embarrassed by the compliment. Then his chin came up and the familiar glint of cockiness and challenge gleamed in his gray eyes. "Not bad so far."

Now Stephanie understood the intensity of Jason's normally defiant stare. When she looked into Jason's eyes, she looked into the eyes of a survivor.

CHAPTER ELEVEN

SITTING in Dr. Sim's office with Stephanie next to him, hanging on his every word, Jason had never been so uncomfortable in his life. Now that Stephanie knew he carried around so much bad baggage he fully expected her to pull back—for their baby's sake as well as for her own.

Instead, both Stephanie and Dr. Sim were looking at him as if he were some kind of dragon-slayer.

He hadn't done anything special.

Although he had to admit that knowing he had been a part of such a miracle as creating a baby made him feel superhuman.

Seeing that tiny heartbeat had given him a sense of continuity, a feeling of making a difference, that he'd never had before.

He couldn't bear to think of such a fragile life having to experience pain or sadness or disappointment. Seeing his own child had flooded him with responsibility, along with pride and strength and protectiveness.

Immediately a huge sadness overcame him as he thought of his world without his baby in it. Still, his mistake with the condom hadn't given Stephanie a chance to pick her own time, or her own father for her child—their child. And now she knew that having his baby came with so many risks, known and unknown.

He tried to phrase his most urgent worry diplomatically, so as not to infringe into Dr. Sim's territory. The effort was new for him. He'd never bothered with such niceties before.

"Is there anything about Stephanie's case that gives you concern?" he asked. If Dr. Sim was any kind of physician she would say yes.

"There are a few details we need to keep an eye on." Dr. Sim passed his test. "Stephanie, your blood pressure is creeping up. So start moderate exercise, although no yoga right now. We want to keep your uterus as stable as possible. Lots more leafy vegetables, lots less processed foods."

"So no more pizza?" Jason clarified.

"No more pizza," Dr. Sim agreed, while Stephanie groaned. "Stephanie, you'll want to hold off on medication as long as possible. With the right attitude you can do it. I know that telling you to reduce your stress is about as useless as telling you to stop breathing, but try. Do whatever makes you happy. Take long, leisurely walks. Meditate. Knit. Go to movies together. Jason, give her an occasional back-rub. Now's your time to be pampered, Stephanie. Enjoy it and take full advantage of it—for your baby's health as well as your own."

She paused, took a long look at Jason, then looked back to Stephanie. "For conditions like this, I often prescribe frequent sex. It seems to be the most effective solution for many women."

"I can see the benefits there." Jason kept his tone purely professional while his mind raced in purely personal ways. He took a sideways glance at Stephanie. What did she think?

She looked a bit paler than usual, with her hands clasped tightly in her lap.

Sadness and worry layered over a wistful cast said it all. Now that she knew about him, she couldn't bring herself to have him. And she didn't even know the worst of it. She knew why his brother had died, but not how. When she found out, Stephanie would never again want him in her bed.

The idea of never again tracing her spine with his fingertips, leaving butterfly kisses on her neck and between her breasts, of never again feeling her hands on his bare skin, was almost unbearable.

He had to make physical contact—touch her, feel her. He had to do something—anything—to tell her he would be there for her and for their baby in every way he could. Would she accept him if he reached over and folded her hand in his? Would she welcome his comfort or resent his presumption?

He took the chance and held his hand out to her. For a moment she hesitated and rejection pierced him. Then she put her cold hand into his warm one and folded her fingers around his.

"Are you labeling this a high-risk pregnancy?" she asked. Her voice quivered.

He wanted to reassure her, but given the facts he couldn't. They both knew Dr. Sim's answer.

"You're on the borderline. Let's give it a week or so and we'll check everything again. Cut down on the salt, even the salted crackers in the morning. No caffeine. No carbonated drinks. Plenty of water—at least eight glasses a day. More if you can manage it." She made notations on her chart. "Jason, I need you to take her vitals throughout the day. I'm writing down a maximum heart-rate and blood pressure. If she exceeds this she must immediately stop what she is doing and lie down, feet up. And call me so we can reevaluate the situation." She scribbled numbers on a script pad. "If you consistently exceed these numbers I'll have to order some drastic rest time."

"Bed rest?"

"I try to avoid bed rest for you Type A personalities. The enforced stillness seems to promote a nervous condition that requires medication, and I want to avoid that if possible. But, Stephanie, I am very serious about getting this blood pressure down. I'm worried about your hypertension. Understand?"

"I understand."

"And, Jason, I'm sure you're aware that doctors make the worst patients. I'm counting on you to watch over her. Be a calming influence. Take good care of her."

"Absolutely." He ignored Stephanie's snort of laughter, although he was glad to see her smile. It was the first since she'd put away her ultrasound images. He had never noticed how often she smiled until she didn't.

As they left the office Jason wanted to pick Stephanie up and carry her as carefully, as if she were a porcelain egg. Or at least find her a wheelchair. But Dr. Sim had recommended walking.

Stephanie took off at her normal fast clip, her flats slapping on the tile floor. It was how they all walked in the hospital, regretting the time spent getting from here to there since it took away from patient time.

"Hey, Dr. Montclair, slow down there." He

caught up to her, putting a protective hand on her arm. "We've got a few things to discuss before we get back to our offices. We can walk and talk at the same time, right?" He kept his tone low and soothing, overly conscious of her blood pressure.

"I'm not a crying toddler that needs baby-talk to calm me, Jason. I'm already feeling weird, like my body is out of control. Don't make me feel any worse. Just talk in your normal voice, okay?"

Great. His first attempt at being a calming influence and he'd already blown it.

Should fatherhood be this difficult even before the baby was born? He tried again. "Why don't I come over and cook for you? I'd suggest a restaurant, but eating out is not a good way to avoid salt."

"Add a back-rub to that offer and I accept." She reached out and put her hand on his arm. "Sorry I'm so jumpy. I'm a bit anxious."

"About the high blood pressure thing—?"

"How many points does worrying about blood pressure add to my blood pressure?"

They both looked at each other and laughed, appreciating the irony. Jason was glad to see color returning to her face. "Guess I'll have to make that back-rub extra-strength."

"On second thought, I'm not sure your hands

on me will lower my numbers." She cast him a wry look.

He could interpret that in so many ways. Instead, he asked the question burning in his conscience. "Are you okay about this baby?"

"What do you mean?"

They stopped at the bank of elevators but neither of them pushed the button.

"I know you weren't ready for all this."

"Jason, if people waited until they were ready to have babies humans would have become extinct eons ago." She'd given this a lot of thought in those first few days of knowing. "The thought of having a baby was overwhelming—at least for me. If I had waited until I was ready—waited until I was sure—I may have missed out on motherhood. And that concept makes me incredibly sad." She stopped walking and turned to face him. "This baby is the best thing that has ever happened to me."

"Me, too," he said. "Me, too."

Stephanie had never heard such tenderness in Jason's voice. She only wished she'd heard joy, too. Without thinking, she touched the back of his hand. The familiar tingle raced up her arm, but this time she felt more than sexual attraction. Or was she just imagining what she wanted to feel?

The elevator dinged and the doors opened, exposing their moment to a dozen staring people.

He shifted away—a subtle movement but enough to break their connection.

After watching floor numbers tick by with the rest of the crowd, they stepped off the elevator in silence, going in opposite directions toward their own offices.

Still shivers raced down Stephanie's spine. She'd bet if she turned around right then she would see Jason watching her walk away. Resisting the temptation to take a backward glance, she worked on her professional demeanor, getting her emotions back under control. She had a department to run.

She couldn't help herself. She looked.

Yes, there he was, watching.

He lifted his hand in acknowledgement while his eyes complimented her. But a ghost of melancholy still hung over him.

Stephanie sighed as she turned away. Jason had never asked for this baby, either. But he was too noble to walk away.

In an ideal world love would bind them together instead of obligation.

She thought back on how different Jason was with her. The way he showed her the wicked sense of humor that he hid from the rest of the world.

The way he worried about what she thought, how she felt. His acts of kindness—like the shoes she now wore. The tenderness in his touch and the glistening in his eyes. Surely that was love for both her and their baby? How could she make him realize it?

Tonight. She would connect with him in a way he understood, in the most intimate way a woman could connect with a man.

But she had the rest of the afternoon to get through first, and that included being the Director of Pediatric Diagnostics.

She was strongly reminded of that as she saw that Dr. Phillips waited for her in the anteroom of her office.

"Is everything all right?" Dr. Phillips asked as Stephanie entered her office suite.

"Everything is fine." She gave both Dr. Phillips and Marcy a smile that started as reassuring but turned to joyous as she thought about the tiny life within her.

Marcy gave her a discreet thumbs-up.

"It's good to see you happy, Dr. Montclair," was all Dr. Phillips said. A nice, non-probing acknowledgement that Stephanie appreciated to the fullest.

"Tell me about the teleconference."

Stephanie invited Dr. Phillips in and gestured to

a chair. If this went well, it would be Dr. Phillips's first grant-funded project. Stephanie shared her enthusiasm.

"The teleconference went well. Our application for the grant is looking good. We have the facilities to do the study, which was one of my biggest worries, and we have the credentials. But after the conference, as the Mayo Clinic sponsor discussed our application with me via a private phone call, he said something curious. He said he'd expected Dr. Drake's name to be on the application, but perhaps the rumors were true and he would be reserving a space for Dr. Drake in the Mayo Clinic labs instead. When I asked him to clarify, he said perhaps he'd spoken prematurely. Does that make sense to you?"

Poaching doctors was not unheard of. The best and brightest were promised money, titles, facilities, accolades—whatever their egos needed to entice them. Stephanie had originally acquired Jason from a larger hospital by promising him autonomy, giving him a Senior Fellow position and a team of his own to lead in the Diagnostics Department. Now she'd taken that autonomy away.

After thanking Dr. Phillips for both the work toward the grant and the insider information, she shut her office door.

Could Jason think the Mayo Clinic wanted him more than Sheffield Memorial did? More than she did?

If so, she would have to show him how wrong he was.

From the moment he saw the image on the ultrasound monitor Jason couldn't stop himself from loving his child—no matter how hard he tried to fight it.

He found it reassuring that his child would have a whole family of love—at least from Stephanie's side of the family.

What would life be like, growing up surrounded by love? His child would never know the fear of insecurity *he* had grown up with.

He would be a terrible husband and an even worse full-time father. What did he know about being part of a family?

He was too closed off, too remote. He didn't need the world to tell him. He knew. A child needed to be shown warmth and affection. A child needed to be shown love. All the books said so. But they didn't tell him how to show it. That was something a person was supposed to know instinctively. That was where he failed.

He would not be like his mother. He would let go for the good of his child.

It was the only practical thing to do.

He only wanted one more night for his memories.

Jason had let himself into Stephanie's apartment and was sautéing onions when she walked in.

She came up and sniffed. "Smells great."

"Thanks." He soaked up her approval like a mop soaked up spilled milk.

She glowed with a sense of inner peace and happiness. The radiance made her more beautiful than she'd ever been.

Sexy. He could handle sexy.

He directed his mind to think sexual attraction instead of soulful bonding. Replaying their nights of passion in his mind, he itched to reach up and release the hairband that held back her long, silky waterfall, to bury his nose in the smell, to run his fingers through the strands.

He shifted his weight, trying to find a more comfortable stance.

She pointed to the dishtowel thrown over his shoulder. "You domesticate very well."

"Don't let the sheep's clothing fool you. I'm still a wolf underneath." He leered at her, trying to put the right attitude on the evening.

"I like wolves—especially wolves in faded T-shirts, worn blue jeans and scuffed biker boots." She gave him a come-hither smile like the ones she'd enticed him with this summer. "You look like every woman's fantasy of the boy next door."

He tried to ignore the look of hopefulness in her eyes, the optimism that there might be more between them.

Turning away, he served two plates and set them on the table. "Let's eat."

Stephanie should have expected the pulling back she sensed from Jason. After his revelations in Dr. Sim's office he was probably feeling exposed. And exposed meant unsafe in the world he'd come from.

She would do her best to show him he was safe with her.

But how could she get under that thick skin of his? Sex and medicine were Jason's only acknowledged passions.

A gentle approach wouldn't work with Jason, so she decided on shock treatment. "Totally in the name of medicine, I think we should follow doctor's orders and have sex."

She'd expected a snappy response, but got a probing stare instead.

"Why?"

Stephanie felt as if she was performing microsurgery. Any slip of the scalpel would be disastrous.

"It's what I need, Jason." *And what you need, too,* she wanted to say. But now she understood. Jason couldn't admit need. To need was to be weak, and in the world that formed him the weak didn't survive.

Could she show him he didn't have to live that way any longer?

"Maybe I'm being totally selfish here, Jason, but can't you give me tonight?"

At first she thought he wouldn't answer, but finally he sighed, as if he had been defeated. "Yes, we can have tonight."

Stephanie forced cheerfulness. "I choose not to be insulted by that less than enthusiastic reply. You can make it up to me by giving me a night to remember."

He focused on her mouth, then her eyes. His own eyes darkened with passion. "I want to do that." Then a ghost of hesitation skittered across his face. "Are you sure you're up to it?"

"Absolutely. For health reasons, remember?" she said, making them both grin, although his mouth stayed tight at the corners.

She wouldn't give him a chance to second-guess this.

She led him over to the faux fur rug in front of the fireplace—the rug she'd bought just for the two of them.

She started with his T-shirt, peeling the hem up and over his head. Running her hands along his muscled arms raised chill bumps as his nipples peaked. Hers did the same in response.

He groaned, deep in his throat. It turned into a sexy growl as she put her mouth on the sensitive bend between his neck and shoulder, feeling his pulse beat through her lips as she kissed her way up to his jawline.

"Touch me, Jason."

"Stephanie..." He said it like a whispered prayer. His lips traced her cheek before meeting her lips. His kiss was thorough, possessive, and went on forever. Stephanie leaned against him as her knees started to tremble with the realization of how much she loved this man.

Tonight she was his lover—both the woman who made love to him and the woman who loved him.

His large hands bracketed her shoulders while his eyes stared into hers as if he were memorizing what he saw there.

"My dress..." Stephanie resented the thick material that separated their bodies. "Help me take it off."

Jason was already unfastening the tiny closure in the back as she breathed the words. Then he pulled it over her head and she stood before him in her bra and panties.

She stepped out of her ballet flats as he pushed off one boot, then the other, never breaking eye contact, wordlessly assuring him this was what she wanted.

His hands glided down her body, following her curves.

"So beautiful," he whispered. "So damn beautiful."

His compliment made her blush.

She leaned toward him, pulled in by the passion in his eyes.

Throat too thick to respond, she smiled, feeling beautiful, and reached out to trace the upturned crease of his lips.

"You make me so hot for you when you blush for me." He rubbed her flushed cheekbone with this thumb.

"You're the only one I do it for." It was true. Jason was the only man who could make her lose her composure.

He caught her hand, brought her fingers to his

lips and kissed them, one by one, while his other hand stroked her spine.

Then they explored each other's bodies as if they'd never touched each other before. Jason echoed her movements, first the jaw, then the throat, then the collarbone and shoulders.

Impatient, she pulled at the button of his jeans, frustrated when her clumsy fingers couldn't free him.

In a quick move he unbuttoned, unzipped and stepped free of his jeans, taking off his socks with them.

She sucked in her breath. He was so magnificent. All his angles and planes overlaid with muscle.

Slowly and thoroughly he traced her belly and the line of her hips, admiring her lush curves.

His hands grew adventurous, exploring her new silhouette. Suddenly, self-conscious, she feebly pushed at him. "I feel so fat." She wanted to move his palm away when his hand drifted down to explore the roundness of her belly.

"No, you feel so feminine." His voice rumbled deep next to her ear. He dropped to his knees. "Thank you for our child." He covered her abdomen with kisses.

Be well, she told their baby.

Stephanie sensed a contented fullness within her, as if her child were reassuring her.

Her hands threaded through Jason's hair as he pushed down her panties.

He ran his hands along the length of her thighs. "You've got the longest, most gorgeous legs I've ever seen."

She knelt down and guided his hands to the clasp of her bra.

He unsnapped and pulled it free, dropping it before cupping a swollen breast in each hand.

His warm hands gently tested their new weight before his mouth covered one pebbled nipple while his thumb circled the other.

Instinctively she arched back against him as he gave her pleasure. He was so warm, so real, and so very much hers.

His warmth went beyond flesh and blood to penetrate her heart. Yes, there was no doubt she loved him.

As he suckled and rubbed she felt the ripples start, then build, each wave racing over the other one. When she came, she cried out his name in a voice so full of passion she didn't recognize herself.

He held her as she trembled, pressing his hard chest to her throbbing breasts.

Still she wanted him to fill her. "More."

Gently, reverently, he pulled her hair free and spread it around her shoulders. "We've got all night."

"I want you now." She wanted to touch him, to explore every inch of his body. She pushed against his shoulders. "Let me."

In that way he had of knowing her desires, he stretched out on the rug. She followed him down, straddling him. Her hands started at his shoulders, then spread over the breadth of his chest. She walked her fingers down his abdomen, tracing the outline of each muscle. He held himself statue-still, his eyes searching, wanting. She longed to give him what he sought, glorying in the knowledge that she loved him with every cell in her body and every wisp of her soul.

By the time Stephanie got to Jason's pelvic bone they both shook with desire. As she reached lower she marveled at how her long, tapered fingers looked so delicate and graceful against his skin.

"Look at us—how we fit so perfectly together." Ever so slowly she lowered herself, taking in all the sensations making love to Jason created within her.

"Yes, Stephanie, yes." Jason lifted his hips to meet her, restraint evident in every quivering muscle. "You are my bliss."

He ran his hands through her hair, creating a veil around them both. She felt treasured, cherished and revered as he looked into her eyes, his own gray eyes dark with passion.

The rhythm climbed to a crescendo as they shuddered and cried out together. Throbbing pleasure radiated from her womb throughout her body in pulses so strong she lost all control.

Afterward, Jason's breath came gulping and heavy, as if he'd just run five miles, while hers came in quick pants. As they lay together, spent, relaxed, all her pent-up emotions broke free.

"Stephanie?" Jason wrapped his arms around her, pulling her into him, holding her close to him as tears coursed down her cheeks.

"They're good tears," she assured him.

The concern in his eyes turned to cocky pride.

She settled back into his arms, head snuggled against his chest, and basked. The only thing that could make this moment more perfect was an exchange of whispered love words between them.

What they shared between them—the depth, the intensity—meant Jason loved her, too. Didn't it?

Jason had expressed more raw emotion tonight than he had in their whole time put together. Through his hands, through his eyes, through the tenderness and intensity of his mouth.

Still, she needed to hear it. To know it. To be sure they shared that between them. Then she'd know that together they could overcome any obstacles in their relationship.

Maybe she was being unfair, expecting him to say it first. She gathered her courage and drew in a breath, "Jason, I—"

Jason flexed his hard abs to pull himself into a sitting position and held up his hand, stopping her mid-sentence. "I know. You're right. It's getting late."

Being doused with cold water wouldn't have given her a greater shock.

What had happened to the synchronicity they always shared?

Then he pulled his shirt on over his head and rolled to his feet, a perfect coordination of muscle fiber and nerve synapses. Strong. Sleek. Graceful.

After a quick trip to her bathroom he came out looking like a man who hadn't made sweet love only seconds before.

His stance was stiff. His jaw tense. His eyes bland.

No, there was sadness behind that flat gaze of his.

"Walk me to the door so you can lock it behind me."

Suddenly Stephanie felt very naked. A chill

erased all the lovely relaxation that had overtaken her body.

As she meekly followed him, she tried to force her befuddled brain to think.

He had almost slipped through the door before she said, "Jason, I love you."

All color drained from his face. His throat convulsed as the muscle in his jaw jumped.

"Thank you." He pulled the door closed behind himself.

CHAPTER TWELVE

THANK YOU? What was that supposed to mean?

Stephanie scrubbed the toilet using Jason's toothbrush. Her cleaning frenzy was the only thing that kept her from giving in to a need to break things. One fragile relationship shattered to pieces had made enough mess for one night.

No matter how much she might want to indulge in a fit of hysterical crying, she had to keep it together for the sake of the baby. It was a good thing Dr. Sim wasn't around with her blood pressure cuff at the moment. Stephanie was certain her numbers would have been sky-high.

She couldn't believe she'd blurted out that she loved him, just like that.

What had she expected? Some kind of fairytale moment where he instantly declared his love for her, too?

Yes. That was what she had hoped for. Instead Jason had acted in character, with an extra dose of politeness added in.

She felt so foolish. And so abandoned.

How was she supposed to face him in the morning?

How had she let her imagination run away with her? In just a few short days she'd gone from feeling confident about raising her child on her own to thinking they could all be a full-fledged family.

She would like to blame her foolish thinking on hormones. Instead she had to blame it on love.

Yes. She loved Jason Drake. But he'd never promised her anything more than a good time, and then, when he found out about the baby, to be a real father to her child.

So much for her nebulous dreams of mommy, daddy and baby make three.

How would she handle tomorrow? And the day after that and the day after that?

She would act as if tonight had never happened. Business as usual. Professional all the way.

She dropped the toothbrush into the trash, determined to spend the rest of the night re-dreaming her dreams, restructuring her personal life and editing Jason Drake out of the picture.

If her heart didn't break first.

Professionalism. Some days it wasn't all it was cracked up to be. Stephanie faked it, willing herself to keep reading her email even though she could sense Jason standing outside her office door. If she looked up now too much hope, too much desperation would show on her face. First she needed to gather her pride.

After a few seconds, Jason knocked on the doorframe. "Could I interrupt you for a few minutes?"

He looked tired, drained, as if he'd used up the last of his energy. Maybe he had lost a few hours' sleep over her?

He wiped the weary look from his face and squared his shoulders, bracing himself. That was how he faced the world, she realized.

That was what was different about him when he was with her. When they were together the lines that bracketed his mouth and the guarded look that shadowed his eyes disappeared.

That he now lumped her in with the rest of the world made her incredibly sad.

"Stephanie, about last night—"

"Don't mention it, Dr. Drake. I'm pretending that it never happened—that we never happened. I'm hoping you'll do the same."

He gave a single nod and dropped an envelope on her desk. "My resignation. I'm taking a job with Mayo Clinic."

Stephanie felt as if she'd been stabbed through

the chest. Only years of professionalism kept her on her feet with a neutral expression plastered on her face. "Mayo Clinic has a lot to offer a brilliant doctor. Sheffield doesn't want to lose you, but you should go where your heart leads you."

"We'll always have a relationship. I'll only be a phone call away if you or our child needs me." He looked away and blew out a great heaving sigh. "I can't love you, Stephanie."

Her throat swelled too thick to reply. She barely got out an acknowledging nod.

"I can give you a month's notice. That should give you sufficient time to find someone else."

She scraped together all her pride to say, "Don't let your obligations here hold you back. I'm certain I'll manage just fine."

Blessed numbness finally overtook her. It felt so unreal—as if it was all happening to someone else.

"I have Maggie's test results back," he said, as if nothing had changed between them. "It's a birth defect." His shoulders slumped in defeat. "I can't undo what nature has done this time."

She was surprised to see his vulnerability show. The nurturer in her wanted to go to him, comfort him, but that would be a mistake for both of them, wouldn't it? She hoped her heart would catch up with her head soon. Instead she picked up the paper he'd extended and read through the results. "Do you want me to explain it to Anne?"

"No, I'll do it. I just need you to sign off on her case so we can close it out." He glared at her as if he expected her to rebuke him. "I took the liberty of calling her in. She's waiting in a consultation room."

Was that the role she'd been relegated to? Jason's disciplinarian? It broke her heart that they should end this way. "Jason, I'd like to come with you."

"Fine. Let's get this over with."

They made their way to a private consultation room in a united silence.

When Stephanie pushed open the door Anne looked up from her magazine. She must have read their faces, because she immediately stood.

She glanced at her daughter, to see Maggie so entranced with the purple dinosaur on television that she didn't acknowledge the doctors who had just entered her room. "Dr. Drake, is it bad?"

Jason looked as emotionless as the bronze bust of her grandfather Stephanie had vetoed. "Maggie has Phelan-McDermid Syndrome. From the moment of conception the tip of her twenty-second chromosomes failed to form. Less than five hundred children have been diagnosed, so we don't have a good idea on what to expect."

"So there is no cure?"

Stephanie began to say something comforting before remembering that Anne wanted no sugar-coating.

Jason was the perfect doctor to deliver the news.

"No cure." He glanced down at the printouts he held. "I've talked to colleagues at Mount Sinai Medical Center in New York. Mount Sinai has a team researching the effects of this syndrome. Maggie can join the testing group, if you want her to. She'll get the best medical care and therapy the medical community can provide."

"How much, Dr. Drake? If not for the generous donations to the Maggie Malone Fund and you waiving your personal fee we couldn't have stayed this long."

Stephanie knew Jason had provided a large portion to that fund. His charitable giving was one of the many ways he silently showed he cared. If he could only show that caring more visibly every once in a while he would make everything easier for both of them.

"The study is funded by both government and independent foundations so entering the program is at no cost to you. Since we've identified Maggie's disability, you now qualify for public assistance. And Maggie will have excellent care for a large part of the day, so you'll be able to hold down a job, too."

"What about treatment? Can Maggie get better?"

"No. It's a birth defect, not an illness or disease. There is no antibiotic or surgical procedure that will make Maggie well. All we can offer is therapy. I know this isn't what you'd hoped to hear." He gave her a folder of paperwork.

Anne nodded her acceptance, hugging herself, but otherwise outwardly calm. Still, Maggie picked up on her mother's distress, raising her arms to be held. At four, she was a normal-sized child, and Anne was a slight woman. Anne would soon not be able to hold her like she did now. How would she manage as Maggie grew? What would it be like being all alone, with no one to lean on?

She would find out soon enough.

While Stephanie had her parents and her grandmothers, it wouldn't be the same as sharing the load with her child's father, would it? But then, regretting reality didn't change it. Anne was proof of that, right in front of her.

Anne patted her daughter to comfort her, deriving comfort for herself in the nurturing act, too, no doubt. "Actually, knowing this is a birth defect, I can finally stop chasing a cure while worrying that my daughter's condition will deteriorate. Now

I can focus on how to make the most of my daughter's limited abilities."

She smiled despite the devastating news Jason had delivered—proof of her resilience. "I'll be forever grateful for all the care you've taken not only with Maggie but with me, Dr. Drake. You've made this stay as easy for us as you could."

"Thanks. I'm not generally known for my bedside manner." Jason looked down at his vibrating phone. "I'm being paged."

Saying goodbye seemed to be so easy for him. He gave a pat to Maggie, "Take care, little one."

Maggie turned and reached for him with arms that could not be denied.

Jason took the child and held her close. Over Maggie's head, his eyes met Stephanie's, revealing a bleakness and pain that had unfathomable depths.

Then he closed them tight, gave Maggie a little squeeze, and put her back into the chair beside her mother.

"Goodbye and good luck." He held out his hand and gave Anne's a professional shake, then abruptly left the room.

Stephanie stared, nonplussed, at Jason's hasty departure. Normally she would have made an excuse for him. But with Anne she thought she could forgo that.

"Men don't express emotions well, do they?" Impulsively, Anne gave Stephanie a hug.

"Not the ones I know."

"Thank you for all you've done for us, Dr. Montclair. You'll take care of Dr. Drake for us, won't you? He needs you."

Anne had definitely romanticized her daughter's doctor. Stephanie had proof Dr. Drake didn't need her.

For the next several weeks Stephanie moved through her job mechanically. Although she had worked out an agreement with the Mayo Clinic that Sheffield Memorial would keep Dr. Drake until she found a replacement, she was duty-bound to conduct a diligent search.

Since she'd given away all her cases her only distractions were routine paperwork and finding a replacement for Jason. *There can never be a replacement for Jason,* her heart repeated again and again as she sorted through résumés.

But she had no other choice, did she?

At least she'd found a highly competent new cardiologist, so they were fully staffed, even a bit overstaffed, at present.

Even though she and Jason passed in the hallways, his face was a blank mask—as if he was already emotionally gone.

The only reminder she had that he had once cared for her was when Dr. Phillips took her blood pressure three times a day, under Dr. Drake's direct orders.

She picked up the latest official complaint against Dr. Drake. They were coming in fast and furious as he became sharper and sharper to the staff. She had bitten back her own prickly remarks on more than one occasion.

She needed Jason gone so she could move on.

And Jason? It was very apparent he needed nothing from her.

On Wednesday, right in the middle of a very long, tense week, Jason's call came just as Stephanie was getting ready to go home and put her feet up. "Stephanie, I need you in E.R. *Stat*."

He needed her? Even in a purely professional context his words struck her.

He would be flying out on Monday, to sign the contract binding him to the Mayo Clinic. Then she could begin to put him out of her mind. And someday, she might be able to purge him from her heart.

Stephanie passed by Amelia's foster parents in

the hallway, their faces pale with worry, their hands intertwined, drawing support from each other.

In the E.R., Jason stood over Amelia, his gray eyes intent and fierce. He acknowledged her with a glance before his gaze darted back to his patient.

"Suspected peritonitis from the rupture of an amoebic liver abscess," he dictated to the nurse recording the case. "We need to do an ultrasound to confirm, and draw blood to see if our patient is septic."

As Stephanie came alongside him she knew just where to stand to keep from crowding him yet be accessible for anything he might need. They had always fit well together in their work-life—and in their sex-life. If only that trait had carried over to their personal life.

A nurse attempted to draw blood, but Amelia struck out, feeble though she was.

"No. Don't touch," she ground through her teeth.

Her blood pressure reflected her distress. They needed to keep her as calm as possible. Amelia had too much stacked against her to add shock to the equation.

"Amelia, look at me," Jason commanded. "Watch my eyes. Keep focused on me and don't move. We have to stick your arm to give you something for the pain."

He locked stares with her while Stephanie held the girl's arm for the nurse to draw her samples.

"You can do this, Amelia," he said. "You *will* do this."

His raw emotion sent shivers down Stephanie's spine.

By sheer strength of will Jason kept Amelia still long enough to insert a catheter and start intravenous pain meds along with fluids and antibiotics.

As the drugs began to take effect, Amelia blinked through hazy eyes. "Where are they?"

"Who, Amelia? Where are who?" Stephanie asked.

But Jason knew the awkwardness of naming people who didn't fit neatly into place yet. "Her foster parents."

"I passed them in the hallway."

"They're here?"

"Yes, Amelia, they're here," Stephanie confirmed.

The brackets around her mouth loosened. "I'm glad. I don't want to die alone."

Jason wanted to reassure her, but he couldn't lie to her. Amelia's condition was critical.

Stephanie stepped into Amelia's line of vision. "You're not alone, Amelia. You have two people in the hallway who are very worried about you.

And you have people in here who are going to take very good care of you."

Stephanie always knew the right thing to say. They were so good together. Jason pushed back the regret he had about their broken relationship just as he pushed back his worry for the teenaged girl on the table.

Emotion only got in the way.

Knowing his slightest touch to her swollen abdomen would bring Amelia pain, Jason steeled himself against Amelia's gut-wrenching cries and ran the ultrasound probe over her distended stomach.

"Hang in there, Amelia." Stephanie watched the monitor, assessing the scan. She blanched at the visual confirmation. "Abdominal peritonitis. You're right on the mark, Dr. Drake."

"I need to talk to them," Amelia said through her tears of pain and fear.

"When we're done here." Deliberately Jason schooled his voice to hold no hint of the direness of Amelia's condition.

He had no time to delay. Every second brought Amelia closer to death. He would *not* lose this girl. She would have a chance to grow up, have a career, fall in love, have a family—do all the things his brother had never gotten to do.

He glanced at his staff. "Prep her for percutaneous drainage."

"I need to tell them that I—" Amelia's blood pressure cuff registered hypotension "—I love them. I need to tell them I'm sorry."

"Push more sedative, Dr. Drake?" an attending nurse asked.

Jason glanced up from the ultrasound he was performing. "No. She's too close to shock." He caught Stephanie's attention. At her slight nod, he knew she understood. *Keep Amelia calm and talking.*

"I should have done what you said, Dr. Drake. I should have told them when my side first started to hurt. I just didn't know what to say to ask for help." Her voice was getting fainter and more slurred. "So sorry."

Jason gave her the absolution she sought. "Sometimes those words are hard to find. But they know about people like us. They understand." *People like us?* Damn, he hadn't meant for that to slip out. *Concentrate, Drake!* He directed the attention onto safer ground. "Tell Dr. Montclair and me what happened, Amelia."

"I was playing basketball. I know I was supposed to take it easy, but it was the first time the girls had included me at my new school. I didn't want to…" Her voice drifted away.

"Seem unfriendly?" Stephanie finished for her. She patted Amelia's hand to rouse her. "Stay with me, Amelia. What happened at the basketball game?"

"Elbow to the side. Accident, I think," Amelia mumbled, so thickly Jason could barely understand her explanation. "What's wrong with me?"

Jason moved into Amelia's line of vision. "Your liver abscess ruptured. The infected fluid is invading your peritoneal cavity. I'm going to draw off the fluid, which will relieve the tightness in your abdomen and give you some relief."

"You're going to operate on me?"

Jason was thankful to hear Amelia's coherency. Her vitals were stabilizing with her mental state. "No, I'm going to use a needle to suck the fluid out."

"Is it going to hurt?"

"Not as bad as you hurt right now. Trust me."

"I *do* trust you, Dr. Drake. They told me all about you."

There was that ubiquitous *they* again. Jason knew it could take months, sometimes years, before foster kids were comfortable with their caretakers' place in their lives. He'd only called one set of foster parents by anything more familiar than their surnames.

"We're going to roll you to your side, Amelia. It will hurt, but it has to be done. Then Dr. Montclair is going to hold your hand and keep you still while I do the procedure. Just stay focused on her and I'll be as quick as possible. Ready?"

"Ready."

Guided by the ultrasound scan, Jason began the aspiration and inserted the needle.

"Ow!" Amelia's blood pressure started to drop again.

Stephanie gave her hand a pat to draw her attention. "So, what did your foster parents tell you about Dr. Drake?"

"They said he was the smartest kid they'd ever seen. Like, scary genius smart."

"He still is scary genius smart. Those traits make for an excellent doctor."

"But they don't make you very popular in high school," Amelia successfully deduced.

Jason could feel Stephanie's scrutiny of him. He didn't have the luxury of redirecting the topic of conversation. He needed to keep his attention focused on the job at hand. But he was sure to hear from Stephanie about being "scary genius smart" later.

Then he remembered. There was no *later* for them. He had too much foster kid baggage left in him for a stable family life.

Stephanie was right. A child needed to know he was in a stable family, that he was safe and cared for. Jason had no idea what a stable family was, much less how to show proper care. Tony's death would always weigh heavy on his soul—as it should, since he was to blame.

"What else did they say, Amelia?" Stephanie prompted.

"They said Dr. Drake's brother was very popular. Always laughing and joking around. A complete opposite of Dr. Drake. He was very charming."

As Jason drew off the excess fluid Amelia's pain level receded and the pain meds finally took hold—as proved by her increased chattiness. A good sign, even if the subject at hand made Jason uncomfortable. But what was a little personal discomfort compared to a child saved?

"How about you, Amelia? Any brothers or sisters?" Stephanie asked.

"No. Just me."

"Me, too. I always wanted a brother or sister. Being an only child can be lonely." Stephanie's wistfulness went deep enough to make her voice quaver. "I was so envious of all my friends who had big families."

He checked his progress with another scan. So far, so good. He debated on whether he should leave a drain or not. If Amelia was septic they couldn't afford any more infection, and an open catheter made her more susceptible.

"Are the lab results back yet?" His barked order sounded harsh against the backdrop of Amelia's and Stephanie's poignant conversation.

Totally focused on Stephanie, Amelia ignored him as she asked, "Are you going to have more than one kid, Dr. Montclair?"

"I don't know." The catch in Stephanie's voice threatened Jason's concentration.

A nurse handed him the report and he began interpreting the numbers.

The lab results confirmed Amelia's blood was septic. For the next twenty-four to forty-eight hours antibiotics would be waging a war against infection. Losing the war would mean death. Jason had done all he could do but wait.

CHAPTER THIRTEEN

IN THE ICU, Stephanie peeked in on the sleeping girl. Her fever continued to rage. Odds were against her, but she was a fighter.

Her foster parents sat tensely by her bedside. Generally with patients of her age visitors weren't allowed in the ICU, but Jason had used his incontestable influence and insisted the ICU staff make an exception for Amelia—for the comfort of her foster parents as much as for Amelia.

He obviously knew the fear of waiting alone.

Had he always been alone because foster kids like him and Amelia couldn't find the right words to ask for help?

She might not have had her parents there for her when she'd wanted them, but they'd always been there when she needed them. And she knew in her heart they always would be.

But not Jason. She was the only one who had ever touched his heart. She was sure she had. But then he'd pulled away.

And now he was alone again.

The idea of Jason sitting upstairs all alone haunted her. She'd seen the devastation in his eyes as the orderly had wheeled out Amelia's gurney. He'd looked so lost, so defeated, so heart-wrenchingly sad.

Had he waited by himself the night his brother died?

His brother had died in a sporting accident, he'd said. Had this case exposed old emotional scars? Or had those wounds never healed?

Stephanie ached to comfort him, but she didn't know how. How would she get through that thick shell he'd built around himself?

Was that what kept everyone else from trying?

Healing was what she did and who she was.

Jason was in need of healing. In need of *her*.

He just didn't know how to ask for help.

She knew him well enough to know he intended to keep solitary vigil in his office. Not this time. This time she would understand without the words. This time she would wait with him.

This time he wouldn't be alone.

Jason's office door was tightly shut, but hard thumping music rocked the shuttered glass walls and door nonetheless. Was he trying to cocoon himself in the music? Wrap the hard rock around him to reinforce that hard shell of his?

A screaming guitar wouldn't stop her.

She knocked out of politeness, not expecting a response.

Dr. Riser came from his own office to warn her. "I wouldn't if I were you."

How many people had walked away from Jason when the going got tough?

"No, Dr. Riser, you wouldn't, would you? Too many people agree with you on that." She turned the knob. "Keep calm and carry on," she said to herself, borrowing one of her grandmother's favorite sayings.

Jason couldn't have heard her over the volume blasting from his desktop speakers. Still, he looked up as she entered, as if he could sense her.

Maybe he could. She always knew whenever he was near her.

I can't love you, he'd said. Not *I don't love you,* but *I can't love you.* Stephanie was determined to find out why.

He cranked the music down and stood. "Do you need something, Stephanie?"

"I need to know about your brother."

A stillness came over Jason as he pulled into himself. "Why?"

Stephanie stood across from his desk, giving him his space. What would he say if she said he needed to talk and she was willing to listen? Nothing. He would say absolutely nothing.

Not the best approach with Jason. But she knew deep down that he would do anything for their child—including talk to her.

"I want to give our child roots and stability. I need to know what to tell our child about her father's family. If she's outgoing and funny instead of scary genius smart I want to tell her that she inherited her sense of humor from her uncle. I don't even know your brother's name." She went for his Achilles' heel. "Please, Jason. Don't you want your child to know more about her heritage than you do?"

"Tony. Short for Anthony."

"What was he like? Do you have a photo?"

He frowned. "No pictures. As often as we were shuffled around, those kinds of things got lost." He rubbed his eyes. "Nowadays I have a hard time remembering what he looked like. I swore I would never forget, but I have."

Very gently, she asked, "How did he die, Jason?"

"I killed him." The earnestness in his voice would have had anyone else believing he was a murderer. Her heart ached for him and the guilt he carried.

But she knew better than to take Jason's confession at face value. Sympathy wouldn't work here. "How, Jason?"

"I didn't love him enough, didn't take care of him well enough, and he died." Jason rushed the words at her and she heard the unspoken emotion in his tone. He castigated himself with each stark syllable, dared her to refute him, braced himself for her to pull back and leave him alone.

But Stephanie was made of sterner stuff. And if he thought his abrasiveness would make her back off, he had another think coming.

Jason would respond to logic where he would reject coddling. But she couldn't stop herself from moving toward him so there were no barriers between them. "Jason, what was on your brother's medical report?"

"I never saw the report. Swelling of the brain is what the doctor told me. Intracranial pressure sounds accurate for the injury," he said, so flat, so clinical. So excruciatingly in pain, as revealed by the shadows in his eyes.

She couldn't help herself. She reached out to him. "What happened?"

"He played baseball for the high school team."

Jason walked past her avoiding her touch, then looked out his window, as if he could see the past if he stared hard enough. "Tony was really good. I wasn't at the game, but I was told he was stealing third base and a wild throw caught him in the temple. He was out unconscious for a few minutes, but then said he was fine. He finished out the game."

"So the coach should have sent him to the emergency room?"

"No. I should have. I was responsible for him." Jason brushed his hand down his face. "He said it was just a headache. It was my girlfriend's twenty-first birthday—a big night for her. So I left him sleeping on the couch in front of the TV. That's where I found him the next morning when I came in. He never woke up."

"I remember you said he was fourteen. You couldn't have been much older yourself."

This time when she put her hand on his arm he didn't shrug it away. Instead, he leaned toward her, ever so slightly, but close enough for her to feel the heat coming off his skin.

"Old enough. I'd just turned eighteen a few months earlier, so I had just been released from the foster care system. I was finishing up my last year in high school during the day and waiting tables at night. I found a couple of guys who would share their apartment, so I petitioned the court and got Tony out of the foster care system." He rubbed his face, then met her eyes, unblinking. "I thought I was saving Tony from a neglectful family. Instead I put him with a worse one—with me. The foster home where he was staying wasn't that great, but I'm fairly sure the foster couple wouldn't have let him die because they had a hot date." He turned from her to stare out the window, shifting to break their connection. "Is that enough family history, or should I dig out more skeletons?"

But Stephanie wouldn't be dismissed so easily. This was too important for both of them. She put her hand on her stomach. For all three of them.

"What happened with your girlfriend?"

Jason was quiet for so long Stephanie thought he hadn't heard her.

As if he'd made a momentous decision, he turned back to face her. "At first I blamed her. Hell, I blamed everybody. But it was all my fault. Lapse of judgment." He drew in a deep breath and let it out. "After Tony came home with the injury I was going to cancel my plans. I was going to do the right thing and stay with him, even though he told me he was fine and I should go. But my girlfriend went on and on about what a big night it was for her. She said if I loved her I'd come with her. I did love her—or thought I did. So against my better judgment I left my brother alone."

"Jason, you were so young. You didn't know any better."

"But I did. The whole time I was undressing her I was thinking I should be taking care of my brother." He laughed—a short, sharp bark full of raw pain. "It's funny how quickly love can turn to hate. I couldn't bear to look at her after that, knowing that we'd been declaring undying love in her frilly bed while my brother was dying on a moth-eaten couch."

He sat down next to her, reached for her hand, then pulled back.

"That's why I can't do it, Stephanie. I can't love you. I can't let emotions get the better of me. I can't get distracted and make mistakes like that."

"So you just pretend you don't feel anything?"

"Not pretend. Control."

"Control? Is that how I should do it? I should control *my* emotions, too? Withhold my care and concern? Carry the burden of my job, my child, all my worries alone?"

"I'll always be there for you, for our child."

"That's right. You're only a phone call away. That's not a relationship. In a relationship, two people share their burdens." She stood and straightened her shoulders. "I'm a strong woman, Jason Drake. I can help you carry your load just like I expect you to help me carry mine."

What could she say to undo the guilt that had eaten at him all these years?

"Jason, do you have the same feelings for me that you had for your long-ago girlfriend? Tell me the truth."

He blinked, then looked into her eyes, all emotions on display in their depths. "No. What I feel for you is so much more."

"And our baby? Will you withhold your love from our child?" As if Tony were whispering in her ear, she knew what to say. "Jason, it sounds like your brother loved you and wanted the best for you. Tony wanted you to find a woman who loves you. That's why he encouraged you to go to your girlfriend. By shutting yourself off you're dishonoring his memory. But you've got a second chance. You've found that woman in me. I love you, Jason Drake. And you love me, too. Denying it won't change it."

Jason didn't know what to say.

Stephanie read his heart. "It's okay if you can't find the words. I've got them for both of us."

For a split second she thought she had broken past his barriers. Then he gave her his stoic doctor gaze and said, "You look tired, Stephanie. You should go home and get a good rest. You've got our baby to think of."

She would *not* give up on him. "I couldn't rest if I were there. I'll do better catching some sleep here, with you." She reached out and took his hand—the hand meant for healing. If only he could allow himself to be healed. "I need you, Jason. Come comfort me and I'll comfort you."

Stephanie led Jason into the conference room and turned off the light. He should insist she go. For her sake and for the baby's sake.

But he was so exhausted. So soul-deep weary.

What would it feel like to rest with Stephanie just for a little while?

What would it hurt to lie with her, take comfort from the feel of her nestled against him? What would it hurt to allow himself the solace of her presence long enough to rest and gather his fortitude?

He guided them both back on the couch barely big enough for one, settling her on top of him. Kicking off her shoes, she laid her head on his chest and threaded her fingers through his. Her breathing was soft and slow and relaxed, the way they'd both learned in med school, so they would drop instantly to sleep, letting go of consciousness to make the most of their short breaks.

But he'd never been good at letting go.

Without reservation, she breathed the trusting breath of sleep.

Stephanie was right. She was the strongest woman he knew.

And she saw into him—saw into the dark places and said she loved him anyway. Unconditional love.

Was that what Tony would have wished for him? It was what *he* would have wanted for his brother. It was what he wanted for Amelia and all the other foster kids out there who needed someone to show them how to love.

In Stephanie he could have that home he'd always wanted. The family he hadn't dared to dream about.

What would it feel like to go to sleep at night, knowing the woman who lay next to him loved him? He couldn't even imagine the feeling. But he would love to give it a try.

Lying with Stephanie like this, he could feel his muscles relax.

He drifted off to sleep, dreaming of the comfort she gave him just by holding his hand.

Some time later—as deeply as he had been sleeping, he had no idea how much later—Jason awakened to the buzz of his phone. He tried to catch it quickly, to keep from disturbing Stephanie, but she'd had the same training he'd had and came awake and alert instantly.

"Drake, here." He listened as the floor nurse gave him the optimistic news that Amelia's fever had broken and her blood count was improving. Finally her body was responding to all the antibiotics they were pumping into her.

Stephanie put her hand on his arm as he listened, ready to cope with whatever news he broke. Ready to support him however she could.

His heart swelled as he realized that by loving Stephanie he would truly never be alone again. And neither would Stephanie. He could give her that.

"Amelia's going to be fine."

Sunshine broke through Stephanie's drawn features. "You did it, Jason. You saved her."

Then puzzlement followed by pain creased her face and her hand went to her belly.

"Stephanie, what's wrong?"

"I'm not sure. Maybe nothing. I'm a little dizzy—probably from standing up too quickly."

He already had his phone out, scrolling for Dr.

Sim's number before Stephanie had finished her self-assessment.

"Dr. Sim just finished delivering twins. She'll see us in her office as soon as we can get upstairs and across the street." Worried about her clammy coloring, he pointed to the couch. "Sit and I'll get you a wheelchair."

"I'm not an invalid, Jason. I can walk."

"You either ride or I carry you."

Her meek nod of acquiescence worried him more than her pallor.

"Wait here while I track down transportation."

"Jason." Her hand shot out to catch his arm. "Don't leave me."

He read the fuller meaning in her eyes—and committed. "No. I won't leave you."

He made another call, arranging for a wheelchair to be brought to the conference room. While they waited she grabbed his hand and pulled him down on the couch next to her.

"I've missed you."

He swallowed down the lump in his throat. "I've missed you, too."

CHAPTER FOURTEEN

WHILE they waited for Dr. Sim's assessment Jason reached for her hand, although she was already feeling much better now that she knew Jason still cared. From the concern that radiated from his very pores and his fervent promise to stay he cared deeply.

As always, his touch made her body come alive—even in her very maternal state.

He leaned down to brush a kiss on her forehead. "I'll take good care of you." The look in his eyes made her feel very cherished.

"I know." She smiled through her worry.

Ten minutes later, she felt grateful for Jason's hand in hers—and not just for the tingles he sent through her.

Dr. Sim looked stern and uncompromising. "So, while I'm not telling you that you must stay in bed twenty-four hours a day, I *am* ordering you to take the next few days off. With your hypertension, you're now on the edge of pre-eclampsia. I'll check your urine and your blood pressure weekly—daily if you feel it necessary. You're almost at thirty-two weeks. We're not ready to start talking about inducing labor early, but in another few weeks or so it may become a consideration. We'll hold off as long as we can."

Stephanie thought of all the unfinished work on her desk. She had been familiarizing Dr. Phillips for just this circumstance, but now that it was here she was reluctant to leave her duties. But she would never put her baby at risk. "I'll make arrangements immediately."

"You'll need someone to stay with you," Dr. Sim warned. "Someone to monitor you."

"I will," Jason said.

Stephanie wanted to hope, but— "What about your appointment Monday at the Mayo Clinic?"

Jason rested his hand on her belly. "You're more important to me."

Stephanie let hope bloom, filling that sad, lonely empty hole she'd had since childhood. "Thank you."

The baby kicked and rolled. She couldn't hold back her smile as Jason's eyes went wide.

"I'll make a phone call to Mike to get myself taken out of the E.R. rotation starting now."

Dr. Sim nodded in agreement. "It's best that you

aren't left alone too long. And Dr. Drake will be able to monitor your activity level, as well as your blood pressure, and insist on naps a couple of times a day."

Jason let out a deep breath. "I should have insisted you go home last night instead of keeping you with me. If you'd had enough rest—"

"Nonsense." Dr. Sim cut him off. "We all knew from the beginning that this pregnancy was likely to have complications." She stared hard at Jason. "You're a good doctor, Drake, one of the best. But even you can't control everything."

He cast a sideways look at Stephanie. "So I've been told."

Stephanie had never wanted to hug another doctor as much as she wanted to hug her obstetrician at that moment. Dr. Sim had said the perfect thing in the perfect way.

"I've got a few loose ends I need to tie up, then I—*we* will go home."

As efficient as she was, Stephanie was ready to leave the hospital within the hour. A worried Marcy promised Stephanie she would call if an emergency came up, and separately promised Jason she would call only to give a reassuring report after any emergencies were already over.

By noon they were both bored. Neither of them had ever sat around doing nothing, and they both agreed that they had thrived on the excitement of a hospital setting.

Still, they tried. Television, books, card games, Jason rearranging baby furniture under her direction—nothing held their interest for long.

And they avoided any discussion of their future—Stephanie for the sake of her blood pressure and the baby, Jason because he was Jason.

As they sat on the couch—not cuddled up together, but not hugging opposite ends, either—Stephanie flipped through baby name books while Jason read.

Finally, Stephanie broke the heavy silence. "Jason, sitting around here staring at each other is not going to lower my blood pressure. The only place I've ever been able to sit and do nothing and feel comfortable is your cabin. There I can rock on your back porch, feed the birds, read and nap for hours without getting fidgety."

Jason immediately dismissed the idea. "At the cabin we'd be over two and a half hours away from Dr. Sim. It's too risky."

"Except for my blood pressure, there's no indication of any other complications." Frustrated, Stephanie plopped down the baby name book on the coffee table, sending a cascade of medical journals to the floor. "The weather is perfect. What could be your objection?"

Rationally, Stephanie was right. He just had a feeling—but, researching expectant fathers' psychological profiles online, he'd learned that most of them had overprotective worries and feelings that had no basis in logic.

Stephanie must have sensed he was wavering, because she played her final card. "What if Dr. Sim is okay with it? Please, Jason?"

Jason felt himself weakening. He could deny her nothing.

A quick call to Dr. Sim's office and an affirmative answer saw them on the road by four o'clock.

But at four fifteen Jason turned the car around.

"This is wrong, Stephanie. You can bring in every doctor you know, but this is wrong. Now is not the time to leave town. Let's go home and you can make me rearrange baby furniture again."

Stephanie didn't like it, but the intensity in Jason's voice, in his eyes, his face, his posture, shouted that his nerve-endings were on edge.

"Fine." She pouted all the way home, and had him move the heavy dresser to three different places before she ordered it back into its original spot.

By dusk, Stephanie had started to cramp.

"It's too soon." Hysteria tinged Stephanie's voice. "Jason, I'm scared."

He thought about denying his own fear. But Stephanie deserved better than that. "Me, too."

She rewarded his honesty with a tremulous smile. "Thank you. Sharing our worries makes me feel like we're in this together."

"Together. It was a word I rarely used before I met you."

"It's a nice word, isn't it?"

"With the right person, it's a very nice word."

"Rub my back while we time contractions, okay?"

Jason had never fought so hard in his life to keep calm and analytical. He made slow rhythmic circles on her back, trying to keep his anxiety from being transmitted through his touch.

"Maybe it's Braxton-Hicks contractions," he said as she began to relax under his care. With his free hand he found the pulse point in her neck, reassured by the steady beat.

Then her water broke.

"I'm calling for an ambulance." His hand shook as he called 911.

The disembodied voice of the emergency dispatcher calmly asked, "Sir, do you have any medical training?"

"Yes." Although all his years of experience didn't seem to be doing him or Stephanie any good right now. "I'm a doctor."

Saying the words helped. He *was* a doctor.

"Excellent!" The emergency dispatcher's encouragement soothed him. "The paramedics are on their way. I'll stay on the line with you until they arrive."

Stephanie laid a hand on his arm, giving him a confident smile that turned into a grimace along with an eagle-claw grip as a contraction embraced her.

"Don't push. Just breathe through it. Try to relax."

Stephanie gave him a look as if he had lost his mind. "Relax? How many babies have you delivered, Dr. Drake?"

Before Jason could figure out how to truthfully yet reassuringly admit to no deliveries in his medical history, Stephanie doubled over with pain.

"Let's get you in position."

By the time Jason had positioned her on a blanket on the floor Stephanie couldn't keep herself from pushing. Panic threatened to set in for both of them.

Jason reached for her hand. "You're a strong woman, remember? And I'm here for you."

"Hurts!" Stephanie's voice thickened with tears as her eyes clouded with pain and her hand gripped his. And then she started to bleed.

What if he lost her? No! Not when he'd just realized what he had. He would *not* lose her.

Control, Jason. Control.

'Even you can't control everything,' Dr. Sim had said.

"She's coming, Jason. She's coming. Take care of her."

"I'll take care of both of you." The hardest thing he'd ever done was to prise her fingers loose from his. But he had a job to do. He couldn't let emotion get in the way. "I'm going to gather up the things I'll need to help you. I'll be as quick as I can."

All the things that could go wrong raced through his mind as he tore through the apartment, assembling makeshift delivery equipment. The sharpest knife. Dental floss for the cord. A entire linen closet's worth of clean towels.

"It's too soon," she repeated again and again as the bleeding increased.

"Breathe, Stephanie. Like this." He leaned down

and set the rhythm, but she shook her head, not focusing.

Jason gave up on encouraging her to breathe through the pain. Instead he tried to break her litany with logic. He had to swallow hard to use his sternest, most confident voice, despite the fear that tried to consume him.

"Listen to me. You're almost seven months and your hypertension has helped the baby mature faster." Jason checked her progress. "Baby's crowning. It won't be long now. Really bear down this next time, sweetheart."

"Sweetheart. I like that." Stephanie pushed, her neck muscles straining as Jason braced her back. Then she fell back, panting. The blood was beginning to gush.

Worry for both mother and child shoved his heart up into his throat. He swallowed it down. "Let's put a bit more behind it now."

"I can't."

Jason could see the muscles ripple across Stephanie's belly. He would give anything to take the pain for her. But sympathetic words wouldn't cut it right now.

"You can." He put her feet on his shoulders and braced. "Together. Ready? Now push."

"Together." Stephanie exhaled and pushed as Jason held steady. "Ahhhhh!"

Quicker than expected, Jason saw his daughter's head emerge, then one shoulder, then the other one.

He caught their baby and held her face-down on his forearm to clear her nose and mouth. He was rewarded with a healthy cry.

"She's beautiful, Stephanie." He wanted to examine his child from head to toe, but he needed to take care of Stephanie first. Thankfully, she no longer seemed to be bleeding.

Did he hear buzzing, or was that the blood rushing in his ears?

The buzzing became pounding.

"Paramedics," a man yelled, and he and another medic burst through the door, carrying bags and a stretcher.

The smallest one, a woman, went right past him to Stephanie with a blood pressure cuff, while the other medic broke open an OB kit.

"Looks like we missed all the fun," the woman said as she pumped up the cuff. Her voice was cheerful, but her eyes were worried as she surveyed the blood on the blanket. She called out numbers to the other medic. "BP one-seventy over ninety. A little high, but not dangerously so."

The numbers reassured Jason. He held his daughter close while the other medic clamped and cut the cord. As she flailed her little arms and legs she felt so vibrant in his arms.

"Life, Stephanie. We created life."

As soon as she'd recorded her reading the medic shifted position, crowding Jason. "We've still got to deal with the afterbirth. Why don't you let me take over here?" she asked Jason.

Jason's first inclination was to balk. Letting anyone take over wasn't in his nature.

"Bring me my baby."

Stephanie's demand overrode all Jason's proprietorial instincts.

"I've done this a hundred times," the medic reassured him. "Daddy, don't you want to take your daughter to her mother?"

Daddy? That was who he was. *Daddy.*

It was the best name in the world.

With awe and reverence Jason snuggled his daughter. She was so tiny, so fragile in his big hands. But, by the sound of her cry her lungs were strong.

Jason knelt down next to Stephanie and put his daughter on Stephanie's chest. "Look, Stephanie, our baby. Our little girl."

"She's got her daddy's attitude." Stephanie grinned. "We did it. Together."

Jason felt his eyes well with tears. "Together."

The other medic said, "Mom, I need to assess your baby. May I hold her?"

Stephanie looked as if she was going to refuse.

Jason leaned down and whispered, "He'll give her right back. I'll make sure he does."

Reluctantly, Stephanie agreed.

The medic examined the baby from head to toe, gently cleaning her as he went. "Estimated weight five pounds and a little more. We'll get an exact weight at the hospital. She's an eight on the APGAR. We need to watch her color."

The other medic nodded her agreement.

Stephanie sat up and reached for her daughter. "What's wrong with her?"

Wisely, the medic immediately handed the baby to her. "She's perfect, ma'am. But her skin is a bit mottled. We'll just make extra sure that she keeps pinking up for us."

Stephanie's eyes widened as her second wave of contractions started.

"Jason, hold our daughter, please."

Jason could tell something wasn't quite right when the medic examined the placenta.

She bagged it and looked to the other medic. "Let's roll."

Very gently, the medic knelt down near

Stephanie. "Ma'am, your blood pressure is dropping, and you haven't quite expelled all the placenta. Nothing to worry about. We're taking good care of you. But Daddy may want to keep holding the baby since you may continue to have contractions. Stay calm and we'll have you fixed up soon."

Stephanie looked past her shoulder to Jason. "Take care of our daughter, Daddy. She needs you."

And I need you. He wanted to say it out loud, but the words stuck in his throat as all the trauma of the preceding hour crashed down on him. And it wasn't over yet.

All he could do was nod.

The second medic took a silver-sided blanket from the package. "It's a little chilly outside, sir. Skin to skin is best, if you want to put her under your shirt to get her into the ambulance. On the ride, make sure you check her color and she stays alert. If she looks like she's falling asleep thump the bottom of her foot. I'll help you check her."

Jason quickly lifted his T-shirt. "Will do."

The medic wrapped a survival blanket around both Jason and his daughter.

Both medics helped Stephanie onto the stretcher. The smaller medic was stronger than she looked.

On the elevator ride down, Jason held their daughter next to his heart with one hand and put his other hand on his beloved's heart. He wanted to feel the reassuring beat, but couldn't through the vibrations of the elevator. "Hang in there, sweetheart."

"We'll be all right, Jason. I promise." Stephanie made a feeble attempt to comfort him—to comfort *him*!—by patting his hand. "Like you, I don't make promises I don't intend to keep. Trust me?"

He said the three words he'd never said to anyone else in his whole life. "I trust you."

Through her exhaustion she smiled, eyes shining.

Once inside the ambulance Jason held his daughter close, willing his body to give her warmth, to give her life.

Stephanie held onto the baby's foot under his shirt, needing to touch her daughter. "How's our baby doing, Daddy?"

He wanted to lift the blanket and study her, memorize the shape of her eyes, the tilt of her nose, the bow of her mouth. But he made the practical decision and kept her warm and covered.

"I can feel her chest rise and fall with each breath. She's got no ascertainable respiratory distress. Amazing for an infant born this early." Jason felt reassured that Stephanie's coloring was coming back. "Our daughter is very determined. Just like her mother."

Stephanie squeezed his hand at that. "And stubborn like her father, too."

This was his family. The beauty of it all made his breath catch.

"I think I'll rest a while, since you've got everything under control." Stephanie's eyes fluttered closed.

He leaned down close to adjust her blanket.

"I love you," he whispered, dropping a kiss on her forehead. "I'll take good care of our family."

The on-board monitor showed Stephanie's blood pressure coming down steadily. But the ambulance ride to the hospital couldn't be over quickly enough for Jason.

Once there, Dr. Sim took charge of Stephanie, while he was instructed to take the baby up to the neonatal nursery.

The separation felt as if he was leaving part of himself behind.

"You saved them, Jason. Both of them. They would have died without you," Mike said as he accompanied Jason from the E.R. to Neonatal.

"Stephanie is my life," Jason said. "Why has it been so hard to tell her that?"

"You've got another chance." Mike clapped him

on the shoulder. "Don't screw it up by holding back."

"I won't."

The next hours went by in a blur for Jason, as he sat in the nursery and rocked his daughter. But finally Stephanie was comfortably settled into her hospital room and Jason joined her, carrying their daughter.

Immediately Stephanie reached for her.

Not wanting to be separated from her, Jason handed over the baby, but continued to stroke her back with his index finger while Dr. Sim debriefed them on Stephanie's condition.

"You had a small tear, probably from the placenta partially separating, but a simple procedure fixed you right up. You'll have no ill effects should you wish to have more children in the future."

Jason watched for Stephanie's reaction. He *would* have a future with Stephanie. He could hardly wait for the right time to ask her—*beg* her, if need be— to marry him.

"That's good news. But let's save talk of more babies for later, after I've gotten used to this one. Jason, what does the pediatrician say about our daughter?"

Our daughter. Frissons of joy raced through Jason every time he heard that. "She's well enough to stay in your room with you, as long as she keeps up her strength. If she'd been full term she would have been a very big baby. As we hoped, your hypertension worked in your favor, giving the baby some extra maturity."

"Look, Jason. She's trying to nurse. Help me with her."

Within minutes their daughter was suckling energetically. Stephanie's face glowed as she watched. "She knows just what to do, despite her small size. It seems she's scary genius smart—like her father."

"And beautifully independent like her mother." Determined to voice his emotions, no matter how exposed it made him feel, Jason said, "I've never seen anything as wondrous as our daughter at her mother's breast. It makes my heart swell."

The brilliance in Stephanie's eyes made his discomfort worth the risk of vulnerability. After all, she had risked her life to bring their daughter into the world. The least he could do was express his appreciation.

Once their daughter was full and fast asleep, Stephanie yawned. "I think I need a nap. Can you put her in the bassinet now?"

"You're all right?" He meant more than in the physical way.

Stephanie understood. She covered Jason's hand

which rested on their baby. "More than all right. This is the best moment of my life."

He breathed a sigh of relief. Stephanie was fine. And he was very, very happy.

Now. He should ask her *now*.

But Stephanie already slept.

Putting his daughter down, he stretched. Now he could examine her, trace her nose and her mouth and her ears.

That was when he noticed she'd stopped breathing.

He'd never felt so on the edge of losing control in his life. For a split second he didn't know what to do.

Then his training took over. He pushed aside his panicked emotions, picked her up and thumped her foot.

She took a deep, gasping breath, then snuggled against her daddy's chest, her little chest smoothly rising and falling.

"Apnea and bradycardia," Dr. Rivers, the pediatrician, diagnosed. "It's not unusual for a baby born at thirty-two weeks to forget to breathe and for her heart to forget to beat."

"But this isn't just any baby. This is *my* baby."

Now Jason understood all those parents with the worried eyes and sharp tones, demanding answers.

"Yes, Dr. Drake, she's pretty special, and she's already a daddy's girl," Dr. Rivers said diplomatically. "Her heart-rate and breathing seem to stay steady as long as she's lying on her daddy's chest."

Stephanie cradled her daughter's little arm that was threaded through Jason's big hand. "What are our options?"

"We have two. We can hook her up to some equipment to help her breathe, and I can give her drugs to make her heart beat until she matures enough to be weaned from them. Or Jason can hold her until she outgrows the tendency."

"What's it going to be, Jason? Medicine or love?" Stephanie challenged with a knowing look.

"We only have one acceptable option. My daughter isn't starting out life in a cold plastic crib, poked and prodded and drugged for weeks."

She smiled. "I knew you'd say that."

So night after night Jason slept in Neonatal. During the day he caught up on his paperback reading, becoming adept at turning the pages one-handed with his daughter nestled to his chest. The hungry little girl was strong enough to breastfeed, which she did at every opportunity—so long as her daddy was there as well. When Stephanie nursed the baby he had to keep one hand on their child's tiny back, talking to her all the while, or she would quit sucking.

"Jason, we *must* see if she will breathe on her own. You have to put her down sometime," Dr. Rivers insisted. "Consider it an early lesson in parenting. You can't protect them from everything."

"Together, Jason. We can do this together." Stephanie proved what a strong woman she was as she kept a tight hold on his hand while they watched their daughter, giving him strength and courage and helping him hold onto his emotions.

The first time he put her down she turned blue and almost brought him to his knees.

Watching her grow limp then gasp for air broke his heart. And there was no doubt he'd given his heart to her—and to her mother.

When Stephanie's parents came to visit, her mother said, "When are you going to name our granddaughter? We can't keep calling her 'the baby'. I've got monograms to be embroidered."

Jason looked to Stephanie. "That's up to her mother."

He didn't care what his daughter was called as long as she thrived. That was all that mattered to him.

"I've decided on a family name," Stephanie said.

Suddenly it did matter.

Not Clarice, after your mother. Jason silently sent her the message with his eyes.

She grinned up into his worried face. "Antonia. Tonie for short."

"But, Stephanie, there are no Antonias or Tonies on either your father's or my side of the family."

"But there is on her father's side."

Jason was suspiciously quiet. She'd thought he would be pleased.

She cast a look at him—and saw the emotion glitter in his eyes.

"Tonie," he said. "Thank you."

By the end of the third week their pediatrician declared Tonie out of danger.

They wrapped their baby up, and Jason strapped her into the car seat of his new sensible family car for the first time. The short two feet of separation almost made him panic. But Stephanie sensed Jason's turmoil and gave him a tight hug, and Tonie kept on breathing, in and out, as she was supposed to.

"First you save me, and then you save our baby," Stephanie whispered in his ear. "My own personal hero."

Jason had never felt more pride. They needed him. His family needed him.

And he needed them.

Before Jason helped Stephanie into the passenger seat he covered her hand with his. "I was so afraid I might lose you."

"Not a chance. You're stuck with me now." She squeezed his arm. "When I wanted to go to the cabin you told me no. And yet, in the ambulance you said you loved me."

"Stephanie—"

"I'm making a point. Love hasn't distracted you from what's most important."

"That's because you and Tonie are what's most important to me."

She looked up at him. "You might as well say it again. The practice will do you good, because I expect you to say it every day for the rest of our lives."

"I always follow doctor's orders." He could deny her nothing—most of the time. "Stephanie, I love you. Will you marry me?"

"Yes! A hundred times yes!"

His kiss was tender and deep, flooding her with love. Neither of them broke it off until Tonie made a noise from her car seat.

"Stephanie, my love, let's take our family home."

* * * * *

Mills & Boon® Large Print

Medical

September

FALLING FOR THE SHEIKH SHE SHOULDN'T	Fiona McArthur
DR CINDERELLA'S MIDNIGHT FLING	Kate Hardy
BROUGHT TOGETHER BY BABY	Margaret McDonagh
ONE MONTH TO BECOME A MUM	Louisa George
SYDNEY HARBOUR HOSPITAL: LUCA'S BAD GIRL	Amy Andrews
THE FIREBRAND WHO UNLOCKED HIS HEART	Anne Fraser

October

GEORGIE'S BIG GREEK WEDDING?	Emily Forbes
THE NURSE'S NOT-SO-SECRET SCANDAL	Wendy S. Marcus
DR RIGHT ALL ALONG	Joanna Neil
SUMMER WITH A FRENCH SURGEON	Margaret Barker
SYDNEY HARBOUR HOSPITAL: TOM'S REDEMPTION	Fiona Lowe
DOCTOR ON HER DOORSTEP	Annie Claydon

November

SYDNEY HARBOUR HOSPITAL: LEXI'S SECRET	Melanie Milburne
WEST WING TO MATERNITY WING!	Scarlet Wilson
DIAMOND RING FOR THE ICE QUEEN	Lucy Clark
NO.1 DAD IN TEXAS	Dianne Drake
THE DANGERS OF DATING YOUR BOSS	Sue MacKay
THE DOCTOR, HIS DAUGHTER AND ME	Leonie Knight